Novan Witch

Nova series, Volume 1

Prudence MacLeod

Published by Prudence MacLeod, 2023.

Novan Witch

by

Prudence MacLeod

Copyright, November 2011

NOVAN WITCH

First edition. December 10, 2023.

Copyright © 2023 Prudence MacLeod.

ISBN: 978-1927478332

Written by Prudence MacLeod.

Taken

The tall woman darted from boulder to boulder, taking cover behind each in turn. All around her were the pings of projectiles ricocheting off the giant stones, and the hiss of energy weapons' fire. She took a quick glance then faked a leap from her hiding place. Several weapons fired at once.

Had she actually taken that leap it would have been her last. She sped from the other side of the boulder and ran to the next. In this fashion she crossed half a kilometer of battle zone. Suddenly there was a shout and a hail of covering fire was laid down for her.

She raced to the shelter of the overturned land transport ship, and the soldiers hunkered down behind it. "Woman, what the nine hells are you doing here, and where are my reinforcements?" The officer before her was huge, and he was chewing on a tobar root. This told her he had probably not eaten for days.

"I'm Lessa, a healer. I've come to tend the wounded. I know nothing of reinforcements."

The big man sighed deeply and spat out the root. "There are plenty of wounded here for you, just behind that ridge. Use the tunnel, it's safe enough."

She nodded and started away, but he spoke again. "You wear two armbands. Are you both healer and dispatcher, Temple trained?"

"I am." He nodded his head sadly. "Help those you can; dispatch those you cannot."

She paused slightly but did not meet his eyes. "Understood." With that she trotted behind the ragged men and vanished into the tunnel.

The smell hit her first, long before she saw the wounded, or heard their cries of pain. As she emerged from the tunnel they were spread about on the ground, one man working carefully, trying to help them. He himself was wounded, but not badly. Spotting the newcomer, he approached. "Who are you?"

"I'm Lessa, a healer."

"Healer or dispatcher?"

"Both, but I prefer healing. Are you a medic?"

"The medic lies dead, just there, I have been appointed. I do what I can, but..." He pointed to a body in a blue uniform; at least it had been at one time. "He wore a medic's uniform, yet they shot him anyway. What manner of men are these Arlens, or are they even men?"

"They're soldiers and desperate men, as are you all," she replied as she took off her small pack and began to spread out her tools.

He watched in envy as she pushed the nose filters into her nostrils. "Have you more of those, perchance?"

"These are the last," she said as she passed a pair to him, "cherish them."

"Thank you, Healer. Now, how can I be of assistance?"

"The grass is soft here, and there is shade. Bring those who can walk, over here." He nodded and signaled to a man lying nearby. The man groaned as he rose, and clutching his leg to staunch the bleeding, lurched toward her. The man's eyes opened with wonder as she cleaned then sealed his wound.

She sang a high sweet note as she held her hand over the newly closed injury. When she stopped he stood and smiled. Her new assistant looked at her quizzically. "You are more than a mere healer, and you are definitely not Borelian. Your skin is too pale, as is your hair. You're not Arlen either; what are you?"

The recently appointed medic was getting far too curious. "I'm a healer," she replied as she pulled the scarf away from the tattoos on her neck, "of Nara Clan."

Her scarf slipped farther than she'd wanted, for the newly healed man saw what she had intended to keep hidden. "Lady," he breathed reverently as he sank to one knee before her.

"A priestess? Forgiveness, Lady, I beg you." The medic sank to his knees as well.

"Granted. Now be silent, both of you. No one must know."

"Yes, Lady, but to know you are here with us would bring great hope to the men."

"Yes, but it cannot be."

Lessa's attention was suddenly triggered by gunfire, and she spun around. Her newly healed soldier had shot a man lying nearby. "Arlen spy," he growled as he kicked the body aside. A communication device fell from the man's hand. "They know you're here."

Lessa sighed deeply. "That is most unfortunate. Ah well, bring me the next wounded man."

The day wore into darkness as she worked. Many were healed, and a few were set free of their pain. She was moving among the most badly wounded, healing where she could and dispatching those she could not help. Lessa hated this part of the job, but it was better to let them die with a friendly face than alone and in pain.

"Lady, you must leave. The Arlens will come in the night. You must not be here."

"None of us should be here. I have a ship coming soon. Hopefully we can fit everyone on board." Just then the call came. "Ship coming in!"

"Whose?" bawled the officer as he and the rest of his men came pounding out of the tunnel. An explosion collapsed it behind them.

"Mercenaries, Commander. They're calling our colors."

Lessa leaped to her feet. "That's my ship! Call them down before they get shot down."

The communications man got busy, and the ship dropped swiftly to the ground nearby. The doors of the small cargo ship opened and a man began shouting. "Get in, get in here now." The soldiers helped the wounded as they all fled toward the ship.

There wasn't enough room for everybody, so Lessa stepped back and pushed another wounded man forward. "I will remain. Commander, take as many of your men as you can squeeze on. Send the ship back for me."

In the end, she and the two men who knew her true status were unable to board the small craft. They fled into the ruined city as the ship shot back into the sky and out into space. They settled into an abandoned house and listened to the silence.

The enemy guns had ceased as the ship leaped skyward. Their former position was overrun and, she hoped, the Arlens believed all had escaped. "What now, Lady? Do you believe they'll return for us?"

"We must believe they will return. Our task now is to remain alive and free until they do."

"Yes ma'am, better dead than a captive of the Arlens."

"Better dead than a captive at all." They both gave her a startled look, but she neither looked up nor offered any explanation. For the next three days they played cat and mouse with the search patrols. The enemy wasn't looking for anyone in particular; they were just securing the area.

More than once an Arlen soldier passed them by when he should have seen them. Only a priestess of the temple could have kept them hidden. Slowly it began to sink in to the medic what his friend already knew. Lessa wasn't just a priestess. She was witch trained as well, a high priestess of the temple.

On the fourth day they lost the medic. He had stepped away to relieve himself and was spotted by a patrol. He fled away from Lessa and her companion. Run down and captured, he was tortured until he admitted there were two others still on the small planet, a soldier, and a witch priestess. The hunt for them was on.

For three more days they fled the patrols, evading them. It soon became apparent to the soldier that she was continually circling the area where the ship had landed to take off his companions. She was still expecting it to return. And it did. On the fourth day a squawk came on her tiny communicator. "Incoming now. Be ready or be left behind!"

The ship dropped out of the sky and landed lightly, but a sudden barrage of heavy gunfire reduced it to scrap in seconds. She screamed a protest and lurched forward, and then the lights went out.

Lessa awakened in the back of a land vehicle, bouncing along. She was bound hand and foot with a blindfold over her eyes. A soft groan escaped her lips as she tested the strength of her bonds.

"Lie still, witch," growled a deep male voice, "Or you will be shot. Here are the rules, keep your head down, and keep your mouth shut. Never look at me. The bounty for you will be paid dead or alive, and I care not which."

"Understood."

Lessa said nothing more and just listened to the men. She recognized the voice of her companion, the first soldier she had healed. They were discussing how they would spend the reward for her capture. Fools! They had put unfriendly hands on a temple priestess. Their deaths would be slow and painful at the hands of the Viceroy's torturers. The temple wanted her back, as did the Viceroy, that was certain, but they wanted her alive and unharmed.

Darkness fell and the machine stopped. A call was made, and a small cargo ship began to descend. As the ship touched down, the deep voiced man shot the soldier who'd betrayed her. "Now the bounty is all mine," he said with a cruel laugh.

Lessa said nothing, and in truth, she had little sympathy for the dead soldier. The ship settled to the ground and the cargo door swung open. A man was waving his arm, urging them to hurry. Lessa was herded along and none too gently.

She held her tongue, for she had seen into the belly of the ship. It was filled with children of all ages and a small dark skinned woman. Lessa had seen dark skinned folk all her life, but never one so black. The girl's skin was like fine dark chocolate, rich and silky, her features fine, almost elfin, and her hair black as a raven's wing.

A hard shove between her shoulders broke Lessa's line of thought. "Keep your head down or lose it, you hear?"

"Understood," she stated softly as she lowered her head. At this point he spotted the crowd in the cargo hold and became angry. "Mortan, what the nine hells of Porapix is going on here? Get these damnable children off this ship right now."

That order was not well received. "Shut your ugly face, Mekkan. This is my ship, and I give the orders here. That woman has paid for passage to Elliston, and she shall have it. Come along with your prize, or wait for another ship, as you choose. We're leaving now."

He turned and stalked back into the belly of the ship. "Hekka, get those cargo doors closed and sealed. Jonal, get her back into space before those Arlen soldiers discover we're here and shoot us down."

The men leaped to obey, and the bounty hunter pushed Lessa into the ship, knocking her to the floor, as he leaped in behind her. He barely made it inside before the door closed.

Transported

As the ship leaped skyward again, several people were flung to the floor. Slowly, they regained their feet as the ship's inertial dampening and artificial gravity systems kicked in. The bounty hunter picked himself up and, swearing profusely, turned and faced the small woman and the children.

"Listen up people, these are the rules. You stay away from me and my prisoner, as far away as you can get. You don't ever speak to her, and never look her in the eye. She will steal your soul."

"That's just pure foolishness," declared the small woman as she gained her feet and placed herself between the children and the man with the gun. Her voice sounded like sweet music to Lessa's ears.

"You think so, slave? She's a Borelian witch. You all keep your distance."

All eyes were suddenly on Lessa as she lay on the floor, her gaze downcast. "My name is Brenna O'Loran, not *slave*. I have resources, and I've paid my passage." She pulled herself up to her full five foot two of height and tried to stare the man down. "There was no need for you to abuse her."

"You have no name except slave. I do as I please with my captive, slave. You may have given him money, but Mortan is a smuggler of illegal goods, and a wanted man. He dare not go within three lightyears of Elliston. He'll keep your money and take you to Dornal Three to be sold in the slave auctions, you to the brothels and them to the fields or mines."

"That's a lie," Brenna declared, but there was a quiver in her voice and Lessa stiffened. She liked the girl's sweet lilting voice and did not want to hear fear in it.

"I'm afraid he's right," came the captain's voice. "We are on course for Dornal Three. I've sent word ahead and the bidding has already started. A small woman, young, and full black is extremely rare. You'll fetch a high price, my dear. Now, just do as Mekkan says and you won't get hurt.

"Mekkan, I don't want her marked. Do whatever you want with the brats, but don't mark my prize." The big bounty hunter just grinned. "Now, just what have we got here?"

The captain bent to take a look at Lessa, but the bounty hunter stopped him. "Don't touch her, Mortan, don't even look at her. She's a Borelian witch. There's a big reward for her."

"You stupid bastard, what have you done, Mekkan? Sweet lord, if we didn't have the same mother I'd blow you out the air lock right now. Have you completely lost your senses? If the Borelians even think we have her they'll force us down and kill everyone on board."

"What do you mean? What the hell are you babbling about?" "There's no reward for her, you idiot, that was just a ruse to find her."

"What should I do, Mortan? I don't want the Borelian clans on my trail."

"Disguise her and sell her for a field slave. We'll be long gone before anyone realizes what happened, but we'll never be able to go back to Dornal Three again, we'd be shot on sight."

Lessa made no sound, but she was grinning. The big bounty hunter had just had the wind knocked out of his sails. His newly weakened energy gave her an advantage, and she planned to use it. She glanced at the others. Brenna was clutching several of the smaller children to her, trying to sooth them, but her brave act wasn't very convincing. Lessa's heart went out to her.

The captain left the cargo hold, cursing softly to himself. The bounty hunter wasn't so sure of himself anymore; this was Lessa's chance to change things a bit. She sat up gracefully, her gaze still on the floor, and spoke. "Bounty hunter."

"I told you to be silent," he roared, rounding on her.

"I need to relieve myself. If you force me to soil my clothing, no one will pay at the auction."

"Fine, keep your eyes on the deck. It's through here."

Lessa rose easily to her feet and began to follow him. "Are you going to release my bonds, or are you planning to hold my clothing out of the way for me?"

He stopped and took a step back from her. He didn't trust her, but she did have a point. However, there was no way he was going to release her bonds.

"I'll do it," declared the small woman as she released her hold on the children and approached them. "She doesn't need you pawing at her."

"Don't let her touch you, and don't look into her eyes."

"Of course."

"I'm serious, woman. I'll be watching as you two come out, and if I even suspect she's gained control of you, I'll shoot you both."

Brenna locked eyes with him for a moment and realized he meant it. "I understand." She turned to Lessa and indicated the doorway before them. "This way."

Lessa didn't speak; she just followed the girl through the door. Once inside Brenna closed and locked it. She turned to see Lessa standing still, head down. She turned the woman, and then gently lowered the trousers of the witch's battered uniform. She flattened herself against the wall as those crystal blue eyes landed on hers.

"Thank you, Brenna," the witch said as she lowered to the seat and relieved herself. "My name is Lessa."

Brenna continued to stare in fright. Finally it sank into Brenna's fear locked mind that the witch was smiling at her. "He will not hear, for no sound passes that door. Neither will he shoot two such valuable prizes."

"You don't seem to appreciate the situation we're in."

"How can I with you so near to me? I find you terribly distracting."

"You're flirting with me? Now? Here? Are you completely insane?"

"Since I first saw you."

"Stop it, Lessa, you fool." Brenna slapped her arm, then realized she had touched the witch. She stepped back fearfully again.

"I won't harm you, Brenna." Lessa sighed as she stood and allowed Brenna to readjust her clothing. "Don't believe all you hear about those such as me."

"What should I believe about you?"

"Whatever you personally experience and know to be true." They were interrupted by a gun butt banging on the door. Lessa sighed then wriggled in the restraints. She lowered her head then spoke softly. "Take me back now."

As they stepped through the door, Brenna was glowering at the man. "Calm yourself. You can see that she is still bound, and all is as it should be." The bounty hunter inspected Lessa's restraints then ordered her back to the place near the big cargo doors.

As he turned away, Lessa spoke. "Bounty hunter."

He spun around quick as a cat, pointing his gun at her head. "I warned you not to speak." She didn't move and neither did he for several moments. Finally, he relented. "What is it, witch?"

"I'm hungry."

"I care not."

"Will you not feed me?"

"I will not, now be silent." With that he turned away again, only to be stopped by her voice once more.

"Water then."

"No, dammit! No food, no water, and no more talking." He was losing his temper and Brenna was frightened. She couldn't understand why Lessa was taunting this madman. She looked away before the bounty hunter could see her.

There was another who watched the exchange. One of the older boys, a lad of about sixteen, was angry at the bounty hunter's cruel treatment of Lessa. When the big man sat to a vid screen and put in the ear buds, the boy slowly edged his way around until he could slide over beside Lessa. He held out a small ration bar to her.

"Eat this," he whispered softly. "It's not much, but it's food."

Deeply touched by this act of courage and compassion, Lessa gently took the food and delicately bit off a small corner then passed it back. "I'm Lessa," she said. "In my lands, we share food."

The boy nodded sagely then took a bite himself. Brenna's heart was in her mouth as she watched them sharing food and water, terrified the bounty hunter would see and shoot the boy.

"What is your name, my generous young man?"

"I'm Micha, son of Kona, but Kona is no more. Soldiers came and killed everyone on the farm. I was hidden, as was my sister, and they didn't find us." There was a deep sadness in the boy as he spoke of the murder of his family. "The girl with the red hair is my sister, Alla."

"A dead man's name is a heavy burden. You shall have a new name. You are now Micha, friend of Lessa."

He smiled and met the merriment in her eyes with his own. "It's a good name, I like it."

The last bite of the bar was now his. "Go back now, friend Micha. Be safe. The time is not now, but soon we'll act. You will not be sold to slave, I promise."

"Nor will you, Lessa. I'll find a way to protect you, I swear it."

With that he slipped back to his companions, who had all been holding their breath. It was some time later when the bounty hunter raised his head. He looked long and hard at Lessa, but her head was down, and she appeared to be sleeping. Reassured that all was well, he returned his attention to the vid screen.

Lessa sat with her head down, focused on the task at hand. It would take most of her reserves, but she saw no other way. "Lessa, this is foolish," whispered the darkness in her mind, "Just leave, and forget the woman and children. Their fate was sealed before you arrived. There's no need to interfere. This could get you killed; then where will you be?"

"Free at last," she replied as she thrust aside the voice of doom and concentrated. She was still for several hours, then, exhausted, she fell on her side drawing deep ragged breaths. As she'd begun her meditation, everyone on the ship had slowly drifted off to sleep. Now they awakened with a start as the first blow struck the ship.

Leaping to his feet, the bounty hunter pointed his gun at Lessa, but she lay on the floor. She was no threat. Another blow struck the ship, and an automated voice began. "Warning, warning, atmosphere leak. Warning, warning, atmosphere leak." It continued as he leaped up the stairs out of the cargo hold.

The captain met him at the top of the stairs. "Mekkan, you festering idiot, you've killed us all."

"What the hell are you raving about, Mortan, what's happening? Who's attacking us? Is it the Borelians?"

"It's not the Borelians, we're in the Zandora Belt." Another blow shook the ship for emphasis.

"That's fourteen hours on a backward course. How the hell did we get here?"

"You brought that witch on board, you moron, that's how. This ship's too big to survive the asteroid belt, we have to take the lifeboats and hope for the best. Come on." The bounty hunter turned to order Lessa up the steps, but the captain cut him off. "Leave her; she's the cause of our troubles."

"She comes with us. I'm not leaving that bounty behind."

"Then you stay here with her." As the captain spoke the bounty hunter went for his gun, but his half-brother was faster. A shot from an energy weapon sizzled and the bounty hunter's body slid back to the bottom of the stairs. The captain turned and ran as another blow struck the ship. A moment later the lifeboats could be heard launching.

The automatic warning continued as the air got thinner. Lessa shook off her bonds, levered herself to her feet, and struggled up the stairs. Lurching as the ship bucked, she made her way to the bridge and fell into the pilot's seat. A moment later she had the ship under control and the atmosphere leak sealed.

Lessa tucked the ship in behind a large asteroid and leaned back in the seat just as Brenna and the kids began crowding onto the bridge. "Are we going to die?" asked one of the children.

"No, Silly, Lessa has taken over the ship, now we're safe." That was Micha.

"Are we safe, Lessa?" Brenna asked.

"For the moment, yes, but there are challenges. Has anyone here ever piloted a ship like this?" Only silence replied to her question. "I see. Micha, perhaps you might be a gamer?"

"I've played a few rounds," he grinned in reply.

"Come forward then, you're our new pilot. I'll show you how to work the controls."

Brenna's eyes were wide as Lessa put the boy in the pilot's chair. A few moments later she felt the ship responded to his commands, awkwardly at first, but then more smoothly.

"Now then, sir pilot, watch for incoming asteroids and avoid them, but keep the ship tucked close behind that big one for now. I need to rest. When I awaken we'll make plans. "Brenna, I need to sleep. Perhaps you could sit here so I might rest my head on your lap?"

"I have to find food for the children." With that, Brenna turned away and left the bridge, most of the children following her.

"That worked well," chuckled Micha. Lessa hushed him then lay down on the floor and closed her eyes. A few moments later someone gently lifted her head and placed a pillow beneath. She recognized Brenna's perfume.

Landed

It was some time later when Lessa stirred. She smiled as she realized the pillow had been replaced by Brenna's lap. "I know you're awake, so up you get."

"But I like it here." Lessa snuggled closer.

"I'm sure you do, but now it's my leg that's asleep. Up you get."

"If I must." Lessa sat up and ran her fingers through her long light colored hair. "Pilot, where are we?" "Still behind the big one, Lessa."

"Getting tired?"

"I'm afraid I am."

"My turn then." She rose gracefully and took over at the console. He sighed and rubbed his shoulders as he stepped away to give her the seat. He stretched out on the floor, his head on his sister's lap and was almost instantly asleep. Brenna came up beside Lessa but did not speak.

"Did you find food?"

"Yes we did, such as it is."

"Enough for two or three days?"

"I think so. Are we going to leave here?"

"Yes, as soon as an escape route presents itself. The nearest place of safety would be Kora Six."

"Kora Six?"

"A large moon orbiting a gas giant near here. As soon as we clear the Belt we'll set course for Kora Six, do a hard burn for two minutes, then shut down the big engines and use thrusters only. The momentum will carry us to Kora Six in about three days."

"Why not just fly there?"

"We don't have enough fuel. We'll need to conserve everything we have so we can make a soft landing."

"Tell me about Kora Six. What will we find there?"

"Ruins mostly. It was ravaged for minerals for many years, but once the mines ran out the companies abandoned it. The terraforming still holds, and a few runaway slaves scratch a living of sorts from the poor soil."

"Can't we go someplace more hospitable?" "Dornal Three is the next closest, and the only other we could reach."

Brenna sank to the floor beside Lessa. "Lessa, I'm so lost out here on the Galactic Rim. There is so much I don't know. Will you help me?"

"As best I can, pretty lady. Tell me, where are you from and why are you out here?"

"I'm from Elliston Prime, a Vice President's daughter. I wanted to do something useful with my life. I came out here to help the children orphaned by the Trade Wars, but I nearly got them enslaved and myself as well. I just don't know what to do out here, who to trust."

"Trust no one until they have earned it, and then carefully. You've accomplished your aim, Brenna. Those children were destined for the slave pens anyway. You've brought them free. Kora Six is a hard place, but they can live free there. It's a better fate than they faced before."

"Is that the best we can offer them, a life of bare survival?"

"Survival is the first step, Brenna. First we survive, and then we learn, make alliances, plans, and build a life. No greater opportunity could you give them. The boys will not die of overwork and starvation in the fields or mines, and the girls won't spend their days as brothel slaves until venereal disease takes their young lives."

"You paint a hard picture of life on the Rim, Lessa."

"Sadly, Brenna, such is life for the poor out here. You're well educated; share that knowledge with them so they can build a better future with their freedom. Help them to grow strong in their new life."

Brenna sighed and allowed her shoulders to sag. She was tired, it was easy to see. "Lessa, why are you out here on the Rim?"

"I was born here."

"I understood that all Borelians were of darker skin."

"I was adopted by Nara Clan of Borealis Prime. I was born on Nova Prime."

With a small hissing intake of breath Brenna slid away from her, out of arm's reach. Lessa sighed deeply and shook her head. What insanity had possessed her to share that bit of information? Suddenly she saw her opportunity to escape their celestial prison. The ship lurched as she spun it about and gunned the engines. A few twists and turns, a close call or two, and they were free of the asteroid belt.

Lessa fussed with the instruments for a moment then opened up the engines for a hard burn. As she shut down the engines after a short burst, she set the controls then slid to the floor and sat facing the now frightened Brenna.

"So, you believe all Novans to be plague ridden. Tell me," she said gently, "do you know the name of the plague that swept across Nova Prime, and the means used to eradicate it?"

"No. It is just called the Plague. It is terribly contagious and fatal if contracted."

"Its name was Rebellion."

"What? What are you saying, Lessa?"

"The people of Nova Prime refused to work for the Company any longer. They formed a government of their own and drove the company people off the planet. The Company then quarantined Nova Prime and released poisonous gasses into the atmosphere. Everyone on the planet died. My family had gone to Borealis as envoys, seeking political recognition. I was left behind in safety when the quarantine began.

My family returned home and perished there. It was then I was adopted by Nara Clan. I carry no plague, Brenna. Do not fear to touch me, or to be touched by me."

At this point Micha slid between them and reached out to Lessa, taking her hand. "See Miss O'Loran, Lessa won't hurt you. Lessa, what do those tattoos mean?"

Lessa slipped off her scarf, displaying the brightly colored tattoos on her lower neck and shoulder. "This one is for Borealis," she said pointing to the largest at the bottom. "This is Nara Clan; this is for the Temple where I was trained."

"What about this one?" Lessa gently removed his hand from the tattoo he was touching. "Another time, friend Micha."

He nodded as he withdrew his hand and rolled up his sleeve exposing two crude marks. "I only have two. This one marks me slave, and this one is the mark of my owner. Alla has no marks as we kept her hidden. The master didn't know we had her."

"You're no longer a slave, Micha. You need new marks now." Lessa held her hand over the crude tattoos on his arm and sang a high sweet note. He hissed in pain for a moment but didn't flinch. As the burning faded, she removed her hand to show his arm with fresh skin where the ugly brands had been.

"Now for a new one." She put her hand on the base of his neck, right by the shoulder. Again he flinched at the pain but didn't pull away. As she removed her hand, he had a new tattoo.

"It's just like yours, Lessa," said Brenna as she inspected the mark.

"Yes, Micha is Nara Clan now. Any member of the clan will aid him if he asks, but he is required to do the same. The mark is both a gift and a burden, Micha."

"Accepted," he grinned as he admired the reflection in the polished metal of the con.

"Lessa, are you saying it was a rebellion that caused the destruction of your people, not plague?"

"Yes, Brenna. That's what happened. That's what began the wars. The Borelians have remained somewhat neutral, and thus have retained their strength.

"The other factions banded together to drive the companies from the sector, and now they just fight among themselves, led by warlords, kings, presidents, and any other title they can think up. This leaves the average person just trying to survive. You called them the Trade Wars, but out here they are just the wars: a completely pointless waste of millions of lives."

"I'm afraid I don't have the skills to survive out here." Brenna sighed and her shoulders sagged.

"So let these children teach you that. These young folk have an abundance of survival skills. Learn from each other."

"Will you not help us?"

"I'll do what I can for you, beautiful Brenna, but only if you will shake hands on the deal." Lessa was grinning wickedly, and Brenna was blushing. Fortunately, her skin tone hid most of it. Finally she reached out and took Lessa's hand. The witch's touch was cool, and it sent a tingle through her. She blushed even deeper.

"Now, is this so bad?" asked Lessa, still holding Brenna's hand.

"No, you're the one who is bad, now stop teasing me. Tell me what I must do once we reach Kora Six."

"First you must hold my hand and stay very close in case there is danger." This brought a snort and chuckle from Micha.

"Stop it, Lessa. Be serious now."

"Alright, if I must, but I won't like it. First we see how things are; if there have been any raids, purges, or other disasters."

"Raids and purges?"

"Outlaws sometimes raid lonely outposts, looking for slaves or other treasure. Sometimes the companies send armed troops in to clean out the squatters from company property. I doubt either of these has happened though. Kora Six is too deep into the war zone for the companies to risk a purge, and raiders often use it as a safe haven. These birds will not soil their nest.

"I believe we'll find poor farmers and perhaps an artisan or two. They will take us in if we give them the ship to dismantle for useful parts and shelters. It will be your task to negotiate the terms of agreement."

"I'd feel a lot better if you would do it."

"I would prefer to remain in the background. I do not wish to draw attention to myself."

"Lessa, what is it? What are you running from, and why are the Borelians so anxious to get you back."

"Secrets, Brenna, secrets that must be held for another time. Now, what did I tell you before when we first met?"

"What? Oh, you said to trust no one until they'd earned it. You also said I should only believe about you the things I have personally observed and experienced."

"We've been talking for a while now, and I'm still holding your hand. I slept on your lap as well. Do you still feel you have a reason to fear me?"

"Yes I do," declared Brenna as she retrieved her hand and sat back, "but for entirely different reasons now." Lessa's laughter was like music echoing through the ship.

For two days Lessa gently courted Brenna. For her part, Brenna was tormented. Here was a witch courting her, and she was enjoying it far more than she would have thought possible. This could only end in disaster, and she knew it. Still...

Kora Six

They had just finished the last of the food when Micha spotted the distant planet on the screen. "Lessa, there's a planet. Is that Kora Six?"

"You can't see Kora Six yet, Micha. That's Kora Prime, a gas giant. Six will be in orbit nearby. Ah, there it is. See that tiny point of light? That's Six. All right, helmsman, adjust course to intercept, three degrees to starboard, two degrees decline, one burst docking thrusters."

"Aye captain," grinned the boy as he flicked a switch on the panel, held it a moment, and then released it. "Course adjusted to intercept, Captain Lessa."

"Well done, helmsman Micha," she smiled as she looked over his shoulder to confirm the course. It was perfect, but the ship wasn't.

"I think we need a healer, Lessa," said Brenna as she entered the bridge. "Several of the children have headaches and appear to be getting sick. I honestly don't feel so great myself."

Lessa spun and peered at the gauges on the panel. She thumped one with her fist and it lit up with a red light. A moment later another red light appeared. "Bring the children here to the bridge, Brenna. Two of the atmosphere processors have failed. The only one producing oxygen is feeding the bridge. Bring them here and we shall pray that the last one holds out.

Brenna soon arrived back on the bridge with the children. She herded them inside then sealed the door. They settled themselves in against the wall wherever they could. It didn't take long for the headaches to clear.

Kora Six was clear in the sky when the third red light came on. "Lessa, honey?" Brenna's eyes showed concern.

Lessa couldn't help but beam with delight at that first term of endearment. "It will be close, but I think we can make it. Helmsman, start the main engines, if you please." "Aye captain." Micha started the main engines and they waited impatiently for them to warm up. "Engines ready captain."

"Lessa, will we have enough fuel to land?"

"We're in a hard place right now, dear Brenna. Do we suffocate and have enough for a sure landing, or do we push our luck and risk a hard landing?"

"Push the luck, Lessa, it seems to be what you do best."

Lessa beamed at Brenna. "Ten second burn, Micha. Ten seconds only."

"Aye captain."

Brenna would normally be concerned that Lessa had not taken the controls from the boy, but she was learning to trust this crazy witch. "Better to go out in a blaze of glory than to suffocate," she thought as the engines fired and the huge moon leaped toward them in the sky.

"I'm getting a headache again," complained one of the girls.

"I know, sweetie, I know," soothed Brenna as she tried to hush the child. "We'll soon be on the ground and your headache will go away. Don't talk now. Just be patient."

The moon was the size of a planet, and it filled the screen as they came closer. Lessa reached over and flipped the switch to engage the shields. Micha was rubbing his temples. "Attention now helmsman, we are on final approach, and you have to land this bird."

"My head hurts."

"I know, but you must focus. Reverse thrusters in three – two – one – now!"

They felt the jolt and grabbed for support as the artificial gravity and inertial dampeners fought against the maneuver and the force of the moon's gravity. "Landing gear engaged. Touch down in five – four – three - two..."

The engines failed and the ship dropped the last few feet to the ground. It was a hard landing, but there were no injuries. They opened all the vents and doors to let in air and inhaled deeply as it rushed into the cabin.

Lessa led the way as they filed down the cargo bay ramp and onto the dry dusty soil. Their haven didn't look all that promising.

"What do we do now?" asked Brenna as she stepped close to Lessa.

Lessa put an arm around the girl's waist and hugged her gently. "We wait."

"Wait? For what?"

"A ship touching down cannot be a common thing here. If there are people about, they'll come to see who it is. If no one comes by tomorrow we'll set out to explore this world."

"Which would be better for us, Lessa?"

"If we had food and water, I'd say explore, but we don't. We need people to come to us and soon." They waited in the shadow of the ship until darkness fell then retreated into the ship and closed the big doors. They went to sleep hungry that night.

Lessa had been sleeping on Brenna's lap, but this time she pulled the small girl into her arms and cuddled her to sleep. Brenna's last thought before sleep claimed her was how odd it was to be rocked to sleep by a witch whom everybody said was so frightening.

Once again Lessa awakened with her head pillowed on Brenna's lap. How had this tiny woman claimed her so completely and swiftly? She'd flirted with, and teased, the girl to distract her from her fears, but it had backfired. She was hopelessly drawn to Brenna and she knew it.

"I know you're awake, Lessa."

"How did you know?"

"I could hear the wheels turning in your mind. Shall we rise and face the day?"

"Why not? So, how long have you been awake, and when did we switch places?"

"We switched when you went to relieve yourself. I've been awake since then."

"Brenna, you must rest."

"I tried, but my mind would not stop. Up you get now, we must go exploring today. Micha is well ahead of us."

"Micha is gone?" Lessa was on her feet in an instant. "Do you know which way he went?"

"He said he wouldn't go far, but he was restless. There's no one around, Lessa, and I didn't want to wake you. Did I do wrong?"

"No, sweetie, you did nothing wrong. I'm just a natural worrier, that's all. Shall we go see if our intrepid explorer has found anything useful?"

By the time they had roused the children and had them all outside the ship, Micha was back. "I've found water, but little else. There's an abandoned mine just over that hill. There's shelter and water, but no food that I could find."

"Water and shelter is a fine start, Micha, well done." He beamed under Lessa's praise. "Show us the way now, for we all need water."

With lively steps, he led them over the hill and down into the abandoned mining operation. It had been an open pit mine, and the buildings sat at the bottom of a large bowl-shaped area. There were several large buildings, plus three smaller ones. The smaller buildings must have been the worker's housing. There was also a pond where falling rains had pooled.

"Did you drink the water, Micha?" asked Lessa as they approached.

"Not yet," he replied. "I took a test kit from the ship but wanted to wait for the result. A farmer won't let his stock drink until he's certain the water is safe."

"That's good advice, my friend. Is that your test there at the water's edge?"

"Yes." He ran ahead and inspected the results. They figured it was safe when he plunged his face into the pool. The rest ran to the edge and threw themselves on the ground to drink deeply. The water was sweet and cool.

"Micha, did you explore the buildings?"

"Only those two closest ones, Lessa. I'd been gone a while and thought I should be getting back. There was no food and nothing useful that I could see."

"All right, let's explore the rest of them."

The third building, the one Micha had not yet investigated, yielded up treasure: a storehouse of rations behind a heavy locked door. Someone had tried to pry it open at one time but failed. Lessa put her palms on the lock and hummed softly. Slowly she raised the pitch of her voice until the lock cracked and fell away.

The hinges were somewhat rusted, but Micha found a crowbar and they were able to pry it open enough for Brenna to slip through. "It's a food locker, or at least it once was," she said as she shone the light around. "There's a few crates of rations in the corner. They might still be edible if the seals aren't broken."

Lessa and Micha redoubled their efforts and managed to get the door open a bit farther. They swiftly joined Brenna. Micha used the pry bar he'd found for the door and opened one of the crates. Sealed rations greeted their eyes. The crates were small, but there was enough food for several days if they were careful.

After they'd eaten, Lessa set out to explore the larger buildings. One was an ore processor, nothing useful there nor in any of the others. The place had been picked clean long ago. "Ah well," Lessa thought, "At least we've gained some time to think."

Two days later Lessa knew she'd have to go exploring, the food was starting to run low. With a bottle of water and a small ration pack in her pocket, she hugged Brenna goodbye and turned to go. Micha sounded the alarm from atop one of the buildings. "People coming in!"

"Where?"

"There." He pointed to a dust cloud slowly drawing nearer. A few moments later they could hear the rattle of the engines. Two old open deck personnel carriers rumbled across the dry landscape and approached them. Micha was on the ground and at Lessa's side by the time they reached her.

"Hello there travelers! Perhaps that is your ship up in the hills?" The speaker was a tall man with a powerful build.

"It is, replied Brenna as she stepped forward. "I'm Brenna O'Loran."

"Murtah, Nara Clan," he grunted in reply as he gently shook her tiny hand. "Is your ship space worthy?"

"No longer, and the fuel is gone. Is there any part of it that might be of use to you?"

"There are many useful parts. Are you willing to trade?" Several others had climbed to the ground now and were looking over the new arrivals.

One of the men grabbed Micha by the collar and shoved him forward. "Look Murtah, look at his neck." Micha's new tattoo was clearly visible.

"Let him go, you fool," said Murtah as he struck the man on the shoulder to make him release Micha. "Who are you, little brother? How came you here, and where did you get that mark? The truth now, for she will know if you lie." He'd pulled a woman forward beside him.

Micha straightened his shirt and glared at the man who'd grabbed him. "I'm Micha, friend of Lessa. I was taken by slavers, as were the others. I got the mark from another prisoner. Her captor wouldn't give her food or water, so, when he looked away I shared what I had with her. She put the mark of her clan on me, to show me as a friend."

"Only a priestess could have done that, Murtah, but he speaks the truth."

"You shared food and water with her?"

"I did."

"At great peril to himself," added Brenna.

"It was well done, little brother. I am bound by clan honor to help you if I can. Tell me what you need, Micha, friend of Lessa. I doubt we can repair your ship, though."

"It's beyond repair," said Brenna as she stepped forward beside Micha. "We're fleeing from the slavers. We need a place where we can live and be safe as well as free. You may have what you wish from the ship. Will you take us in?"

"What, the lot of you?"

"They're children, Murtah," said the woman, "and she's only small as well. We can make the room. I'm Ena, mate to Murtah. We have farms near here, such as they are. You're welcome among us, but the life is hard and so is the work. What say you?"

"We are agreed," said Brenna as she offered her hand on it. As the two women shook hands, Murtah turned to Micha. "Little brother, tell me of this woman you befriended."

"You must not ask of her," replied the boy. "She wouldn't like it, and I've sworn not to tell."

"Ah, dammit, Ena, you know who that was." Murtah spun away and flailed his arms in the air. "If the clan learns she was near I'll be taken and dumped out the nearest air lock."

"Then they mustn't learn of it," replied Ena. "These folk won't tell, and we'll keep silent as well."

"Where did this happen, boy? Where did you encounter the High Priestess?"

"We were taken on Kuris Morn. My father was a farmer there. When the wars came we did what we could to stay out of it. At the last, most of the folk were dead anyway. The Arlens had overrun the whole world. There was one small group of mercenaries slowly being driven back. She was one of them. I believe she escaped her captor."

"He's telling the truth, Murtah."

"All of it Ena?"

"I know not, I only know he speaks truly. Murtah, he's clan, we have to help him."

"All right, Ena will take you all back to the farm. I'll take the others and see what we can salvage from the ship."

———◦———

IT WAS A LONG BUMPY ride back to what was actually a communal farm. There were separate sleeping quarters for families, but meals were taken at a central building. The children were allotted to different families, two or three to each as room allowed.

A small empty building was assigned to Brenna and Lessa. Micha was billeted with Murtah and Ena, as was his sister Alla. "Does she not speak?" Ena asked Micha as they watch Alla silently trying to make friends with one of the farm girls.

"No, she has not spoken since our parents were killed."

"I'm sorry you lost your family, Micha."

"Thank you. They were farmers. Real farmers."

"What do you mean 'real' farmers?"

"You folk aren't farmers, I can tell. I can show you lots of ways to make your land produce more."

"Then you're welcome indeed, young Micha. Ah, here come the ladies now. Does the tall woman not speak either?"

"She does, when she chooses to do so."

Brenna and Lessa were approaching holding hands. Brenna had released herself to the magic of this woman's attentions. She was enjoying being courted for herself instead of her father's station and money. They were chatting happily as they approached.

"So, you do have a voice after all," smiled Ena.

"I do, and I'm told I use it far too often. I'm Lessa, mate of Brenna."

"Lessa, stop it. We're not committed mates."

"Well, not yet."

"Stop it."

"You know we will be."

"Stop it, right now. Gods, you're embarrassing. Stop teasing me and behave."

"Yes dear," Lessa winked and grinned.

"Come inside, ladies, the men have returned, and the evening meal is waiting."

Ena smiled as she led the way. The inside of the building was mostly one open room with three long tables and benches. There was the smell of cooking food and the sounds of laughter everywhere.

Micha became the center of attention as he explained some of the improvements they could make to increase the farm's yield. The men paid close attention and occasionally one or the other would nod his head or ask a question. It was clear the boy knew his stuff.

The women chatted easily, making the newcomers welcome. It was sweet and Lessa was enjoying it more than she would have guessed. Brenna was the more outgoing of the two and she was working the room, entertaining the women as best she could.

Both she and Micha tried to hold the floor and keep the attention off Lessa. It didn't work. The room went silent as the man who had first spotted Micha's tattoo spoke loudly. "So tell me, boy, where in the nine sectors have you been these past two years?"

"Excuse me, what do you mean, the last two years?"

Micha looked confused, as did the others, all except Lessa. She sighed deeply and leaned her head in her hands.

"The past two years, boy. You said you were taken on the last days of Kuris Morn. My brother was one of the last mercenaries taken off Kuris Morn. They had a woman healer/dispatcher with them. She and two others were left behind. The ship off loaded and went back for them, but the Arlens blew it to hell. If you left Kuris Morn, as you say you did, at that time, where have you been the past two years?"

"Two years?" Brenna spoke softly as she eased away from Lessa. "That was only five days ago."

"Five days?" Ena turned to Murtah then they both turned to Lessa, rose from the table and dropped to one knee. One by one the others followed. "Lady, you bless us with your presence. Have you come to dispatch us?"

"I have not," replied Lessa as she stood and removed her scarf. "I've come seeking sanctuary. Rise, all of you, and resume your meal." Slowly they returned to their seats, the conversation hushed.

"Two years?" Brenna was staring at Lessa with wide, frightened eyes.

"Brenna O'Loran, I grow weary of this." Lessa sighed deeply as she rose to her feet. "What did I tell you when we first met?"

"You said to only believe about you the things I experience myself."

"Indeed, and have I shown you anything but kindness and love?"

"No, Lessa, you haven't."

Lessa sighed again and sank to a cross legged position on the floor at Brenna's feet. "So why do you still cringe from me every time something unexpected happens?"

"I'm sorry, Lessa."

"So am I, Brenna. How can I convince you that I will not harm you?"

"I don't know." Brenna still had not melted from her frightened posture, and there were tears in her eyes.

"Nor do I. My heart is full with desire for you, but I won't be the cause of so much pain. Forgive me." Lessa rose gracefully and stepped to Murtah's table. Everyone leaped to their feet. "May I join you?"

"Lady, you are always welcome at our table."

"Thank you, Ena. Please, everyone sit and resume your meal."

"I heard a story once, when I was young," said Murtah, as he sat and reached for his spoon. "It was about a witch priestess who could time shift. They say it's been nine generations since a witch could wield that power."

"It is rare, but it can be done."

"Lessa, did we really jump two years?"

"Yes, Micha, we did, it was the only way to truly escape the slavers."

"So, it's been eighteen years since my birth year." He was grinning widely. "I'm old enough to carry weapons."

"Don't be in such a hurry to get killed, boy," Murtah admonished gently.

"Murtah, my father had no weapons or skill in their use. Two men with weapons came and killed twenty; my father among them. A man who can't use a weapon can still be killed by one."

"The lad's right, Murtah," Ena said softly. "Out here everyone should know the use of weapons. You must teach him."

"I'll teach you farming if you will teach me combat skills." Micha grinned and held out his hand.

The huge man sighed deeply then shook the offered hand. "All right, little brother, we'll help each other. Lady, we will shelter you as best we can, even though it could mean our lives if it becomes known."

"I will not stay longer than necessary, Murtah. It grieves me to endanger you at all. It's enough that you'll shelter Brenna and the children. I'll leave in the morning."

"Forgiveness, Lady, I did not mean..."

"You fear for your family, as well you should. I will not stay."

"You're leaving?" A small hand lightly touched her shoulder. Lessa laid her hand over that small one and gently squeezed. "Please don't be angry with me, Lessa. I don't mean to be so fearful. Please don't leave."

"I'm not angry, Brenna, but I must go. I endanger everyone by being here."

"I don't believe this, Murtah." Ena sat up with a stern look for her mate. "Just yesterday you spoke of how much better things would be with a priestess here to bless the land. Even the least of priestesses, you said, would be such a boon. Now here is the high priestess herself, the most powerful witch in nine generations, and you want to send her away. It seems I am mated to a..."

"Don't say it, Ena," Murtah stiffened as he spoke. "I will not hear that word from your lips. However, you're right." He turned to Lessa and spoke again. "Lady, we're in constant peril anyway. Truly we're blessed by your presence; please don't go. Stay with us, at least for a time. We'll shelter you as best we can."

"Please, Lessa." Brenna's hand tightened on Lessa's shoulder.

"If it is truly your wish, I'll stay."

"It is, Lady."

"You are Murtah of Nara Clan, combat champion of Borealis Prime some years ago. You were accused of cowardice and treason, condemned to death."

"Yes, I am that man."

"As I recall, a temple slave escaped and set you free." Lessa was grinning now.

"Is that what happened?" asked Ena, feigning innocence. "I'd heard it was a priestess in training."

"It's how the story is told," smiled Lessa. Brenna's arm was now around her shoulder. "With your permission, Murtah, tomorrow I will bless the land and ask blessings of the harvest."

THE NEXT MORNING MICHA went out with Murtah to inspect the farm. As they stood on a small rise where much of the land could be seen, Micha spoke. "Murtah, do the winds mostly come from that direction? He was pointing to the east.

"No, most winds come from the west, Micha."

"Which winds bring the rains?"

"Far too few to be sure, but rains usually come from the northwest."

"That way?"

"Yes. Why do you ask?"

"You have your rows pointing the wrong way, Murtah. The way you have it, the rains wash away your soil leaving more stone than dirt. The winds too can carry away much of your lighter soil."

"That has been a problem, Micha" smiled Murtah. He liked this slave boy who spoke like an old nobleman. "Tell me, what is the solution?"

"Plant the rows across the winds. The corn should go at the edge to block the winds from carrying away so much soil. The rows should also go across the grain of the slope so the rains cannot run freely through the rows, but must seep slowly along, nourishing all as it passes.

"When you pull the weeds, don't carry them away. Throw them on the ground between the rows to help hold the moisture in the soil. As they decay they nourish the soil as well."

"A fine lesson, Micha, and now for yours." Murtah suddenly grabbed Micha by the front of his shirt and held him off the ground, shaking him. "What do you do now?"

Micha struggled fearfully for a moment then relaxed completely, laughing. It was a lesson in combat as promised. "I have no idea, Murtah. Teach me."

Grinning, Murtah put him down. "You had several options, Micha. The first is to make a strong point, like an axe, by clasping your hands tightly together. Drive that axe up between your opponent's elbows, forcing him to loosen or release his grip then slam that doubled fist against the bridge of his nose. That or you could rake his eyes with your fingernails. If he's shorter than you swing your arms up and bring them down on his elbows, bringing him forward where you can break his nose with your forehead.

"Since I'm larger and had you off your feet, grasp my wrist and swing both boots into my jaw. If your bodyweight pulls me forward, fall to your back, put your feet into my middle and flip me over your head. Hang onto the wrists so I fall heavily onto my back, driving the air from my lungs and breaking my grip. Now, let's begin practice."

At the end of day they returned to the main house for the evening meal, both dirty and bruised. The others were already gathered. "What have the two of you been doing?" demanded Ena. "Just look at the state you're in."

"Micha's been teaching me farming," grumbled Murtah. "It's harder than I thought."

"Murtah's been teaching me personal combat," exclaimed Micha. "Lessa, he's incredible! If I had known half of what he can teach my family might still be alive."

"If I had known half what you can teach, little brother, my people would be a lot fatter." There was a general round of laughter at that. "Tomorrow we'll work on free style forms. I need to heal from today's lessons before we have another day of hands on practice."

Smiling her delight, Lessa rose to her feet. "I'm pleased that you two can help each other, but tomorrow is a special day. There will be no lessons, just a celebration. Tomorrow I'll hold a ceremony to bless the land." This brought a rousing cheer from all in the huge room.

The next day began with bathing. Brenna was a bit shy about the communal bathing, but there was only one pool in the stream and everybody needed to use it. The women went first, and then the men. When all were freshly scrubbed and gathered at the edge of the green field as Lessa approached.

Raising her arms high overhead, she spoke a single phrase in a clear ringing voice. Her poor battered fatigues shimmered into the brightly colored robes of the High Priestess of the Temple.

Brenna sucked in her breath in wonder. Magic was unknown in the central worlds of her sector. Somewhat bedazzled, she returned her attention to Lessa who was beginning a new chant. All the others joined in the chant and so did Brenna. As their voices grew stronger, Lessa's chant changed.

The others continued with the first one, holding a strong rhythm. Lessa stepped forward and let her robes slip to the ground. Naked, she stepped into the tilled field, her bare feet leaving delicate footprints in the dry soil. The people held their chant as Lessa sang to the soil, walking carefully along the rows, stooping to caress the plants and the soil.

The sun was well past the mid-day before she finished. Still singing, Lessa made her way back to the group and pulled on her robes. Lifting her arms high overhead, she sang a high sweet note. The gathered people fell silent. Lessa lowered her arms and her robes shimmered back into her tattered uniform. She was smiling with delight and glowing with an ethereal energy.

All Brenna's fear of this goddess melted away as she gazed into those loving eyes. Later that night, as they settled down to sleep, Brenna spoke softly. "Lessa, where did you learn to change your clothes into robes like that?"

"In the temple," chuckled Lessa. "I've always had an aptitude for the magic, but I also had an advantage when learning."

"Oh? What was that?"

"When first I was taken to the Temple to become a priestess, I was far too curious. One day I discovered a hidden library; the library of the greatest witch who ever lived. I was able to read much before I was discovered and the room sealed away from me forever."

"Why?"

"It is believed that the Black Witch, who was Novan like me, was evil. They say her evil magic destroyed her and that is why the library is forbidden. It is also why the power of the High Priestess is so tightly controlled by the Viceroy. However, there was nothing in what I managed to memorize that would suggest ill intent, yet it was enough to give me greater insight into magical workings."

"I believe you, Lessa. I saw into your soul today and I saw only a loving heart. I know for certain now you will never harm me."

"Of course I will never harm you, my darling Brenna. May I ask what gave you certainty?"

"It was the way you blessed the land and its people, and especially the way you looked at me as you returned to end the ceremony. I saw inside the real Arlessa and found there was only love for me there."

"Brenna, how I've longed to hear you say that. Snuggle over here now. I want to hold you close while you sleep." With a smile of delight Brenna scooted closer and was tucked into Lessa's embrace.

"Lessa, can I ask you something?"

"Of course."

"What was it like? I mean, how did it feel the first time you knew you could do magical things?"

"Terrifying, Brenna, and it was nearly the death of me. I was quite young. We were still on Nova Prime, just before independence was declared. We lived near one of the strip mines. One of the mine overseers was walking by our home and my small dog ran out to bark at him. I tried to catch her, but not in time.

"He kicked her so hard she flew through the air and landed at my feet. I screamed my rage and hatred at him, and clawed my finger in the air as though to scratch his eyes out. I felt a rush through my body and it seemed as though I was on fire, and then it hurled itself at the man. He fell to the ground, kicking and clawing at his throat, trying to get breath back into his lungs.

"My mother appeared and scooped me up in her arms, breaking my focus. She held me and stepped toward the man who was slowly getting his breath back. 'Stay away from my home and family, or the next time I will not have mercy on you.' He ran away, cursing at her the whole time."

"Oh my god, Lessa."

"My lessons began that day as I watched Mother heal Pekki. She then began to teach me how to control the magic. Once Father heard of the incident, he made arrangements to get us off world before more trouble came calling.

"That, my darling, was my first experience with magic."

"Wow. Lessa, are things always so dramatic with you?"

Lessa chuckled softly. "Yes, I believe they are."

"Then I am in for an interesting life," Brenna sighed softly as sleep claimed her. Over the next number of days the pattern was repeated as Brenna continued to ply Lessa with questions about her past.

"Brenna, are you trying to glean every single moment of my life before we met?"

"Yes I am. You fascinate me, Lessa. I want to know everything there is to know about you. Now stop stalling and tell me about your first day at the temple."

"Yes dear, it was..., shall I nibble on your ear while I tell the story?" she was rewarded with a small gasp as she gently tugged Brenna's ear lobe with her teeth.

"Nooo," Brenna moaned softly.

"Why ever not, my love?" asked Lessa as she began kissing her way down Brenna's neck.

"Because the story can wait, you have other things to concentrate on right now."

"I do? Like what?"

"Like that button just below your lips for a start."

A number of days went by gently. Lessa and Brenna grew closer and one night Brenna caught Lessa by surprise. The conversation began the same way they always did. "Lessa, can I ask you a question?"

"Of course, my heart; are we up to my thirteenth year yet?"

"Stop teasing and wait for the question."

"Yes dear," grinned Lessa. "What is your question?"

"Lessa, do you want to declare a bond before witnesses?"

Grabbing Brenna, Lessa hugged her tightly. "Oh Brenna, are you certain?"

"Yes my love, I am. It feels right, and besides, you're always telling everyone we're a bonded pair anyway. Shall we make it legal?"

"Would tomorrow's evening meal be too soon, Brenna?"

"I think that would be perfect. Now stop fooling around and kiss me like you mean it."

Lessa was more than happy to oblige. As everyone sat chatting over the evening meal, Lessa rose and rapped on the table with her spoon. The room grew quiet as all eyes turned to the High Priestess.

"Hear me, good people. Miss Brenna O'Loran and I wish to make a formal bond pledge. Will you witness for us?" That brought a rousing cheer.

"When, Lessa?" asked Micha.

"Right now, before Brenna has time to change her mind."

"So be it," laughed Ena as she rose to her feet and stepped to the center of the room. I will stand before you and you had better speak truly, for I'll know if you do not." She was smiling and shaking her finger at them both.

The lovers approached and stood facing Ena. "Arlessa of Nara, High Priestess of the Temple, do you swear to love, support, honor, and cherish Brenna always?"

"I do so swear," smiled Lessa.

"Brenna O'Loran, do you swear to love, support, honor, and cherish Arlessa always?"

"Yes, I do so swear."

"Who will stand for you?"

"I will," declared Micha. "They're both personal friends and their love is true."

"Are there any objections?" Ena asked. Her question was met by a rousing chorus of "No".

"Then it is done. Arlessa and Brenna are now mated. May the love between you last forever." Ena reached forward and squeezed their hands. "Well aren't you going to kiss each other now?"

The young women turned to each other, smiling, their eyes glistening with tears. Lessa stepped forward and took Brenna in her arms and claimed her mouth. As their lips parted, a man began to pound rhythmically on the table, another joined in with two spoons, and a young woman began to sing.

Lessa took Brenna's hand and twirled her around the room. Soon everyone was dancing, laughing and banging out the rhythm in every way they could manage.

The party went on well into the night.

A Fading Peace

Three months passed peacefully, and the farm prospered. Micha was now the chief farm advisor, as well as a combat apprentice. He loved every minute of it. Lessa and Brenna grew close and became lovers. Brenna wormed every drop of Lessa's life story out of her, bit by bit. The people loved having the high priestess with them. They even held a celebration to mark Lessa and Brenna formally choosing the title of mated pair.

Lessa healed and helped while Brenna taught the children and helped out where she could. Their time of peace would soon end, for Lessa could feel the approaching darkness. She finally spoke of it at an evening meal. "Lady, what troubles you?"

"Mmm? I'm sorry Murtah, did you speak?"

"I did, Lady. I asked what troubles you."

"You must tell them, my love. They need to know."

"You're right, Brenna my darling. All right then, I will speak. I sense an approaching darkness, a time of great trouble and peril. I don't know what it's about, nor do I know what form it will take. However, I believe I can protect the farm and her people, at least to some degree.

"There is an ancient spell I know that will prevent anyone of ill intent coming here."

"Then I fail to see the problem."

"I must cast it from outside, and cannot return without breaking it. There is a way, but I do not have that knowledge; it lies in a hidden library on Borealis Prime. I must cast the spell, then leave. It is the only way to keep you all safe."

"Stay here with us, Lessa. We can protect the farm and you." Micha was now on his feet.

"No, Micha, my bold warrior, it cannot be. I would have this farm remain a place of sanctuary for you all. I must go."

"I'll need weapons, Murtah, for it seems I'm to go on a journey."

"Hold, Micha. Your skills have increased greatly, but you're not yet ready to take on such a task. You do have the right of it though. The Lady will need a guardian. It's been many years now, perhaps no one will recognize me. I'll go."

"Neither of you is going anywhere. You're both needed here on this farm. I must go alone."

"No, Lessa..."

"Brenna, my dear heart, I cannot endanger you, nor will I. It will tear the heart from me, but I must go and you must remain. You're needed here as well. As soon as I regain the library, I'll find the book I seek and learn what I must. Then I will return to you. No power in the universe will keep me from your side for long, I swear it."

"You're going for more than that spell, aren't you?"

"Yes, my beloved, I am. I must regain the library for many reasons, and the answers I need, we all need, are contained therein. Of this I am certain. This coming darkness has only prompted me into action. It is so wonderful here with all of you, I didn't want it to end, but the time has come. Brenna, I will learn what I must then return for you.

"I leave in the morning, Murtah. Keep everyone on the farm for three days then you can come and go at will. In future, no one with ill intent will be able to approach the farm. You will be well forewarned of an aerial attack. Three days, mark me."

"Three days, Lady. Understood."

The next morning saw a tearful good-bye before Lessa marched away towards the east. Brenna watched until Lessa waved from the top of the rise then vanished down the other side. They were parted and each woman felt a huge emptiness inside.

The sun was high overhead when Lessa stopped and prepared herself. It was sunset by the time she had finished. Exhausted, she lay and rested her head on the ground. She awakened to the smell of cooking food. Micha was hunkered over a small fire, tending a pot of something that smelled delicious.

"You should not have followed me, now I must cast the spell again." Lessa was irritated and hungry, and letting it show.

"Don't be a cross patch, Lessa, I didn't follow you, I left in the night, ahead of you. You said you would go east, so I came on ahead. I didn't want to mess up your spell." Lessa shook her head and grinned.

"Cross patch? How dare you speak to the high priestess of the temple in that fashion?"

"Oops, sorry. Would a ration of Ena's porridge buy me some forgiveness?"

"It just might at that. Micha, I told you not to come. Why are you here?"

"I've sworn to protect you, Lessa, and you're sure to get into trouble."

She settled down beside him and accepted the bowl and spoon. "What of Alla? Will she not need your protection and guidance?"

"Alla is better off with Ena and Miss O'Loran. Each time she looks at me she sees me holding her still and willing her to be silent as our family was killed. She will regain her voice much faster without me there."

"Surely she understands that you did what had to be done."

"She does, but the memory still haunts her. She will do better this way."

Lessa was silent for a few moments, and then she spoke softly. "Micha, how is it that a sixteen year old boy speaks like a high-born man of fifty?"

This brought a chuckle from Micha. "Kona, my father, was farm born, slaves for generations, but mother was high born, captured by Arlen slavers and sold to Master. He bred her to father in hopes of improving the strength of the stock. She taught me high born speech in case I ever managed to escape.

"I kin talk de talk o de farm folk. Dis wuz de talk o dem livin' at de farm. Tain't much hard, ner do sound likely ta most. 'Tisn't sa hird ta ken, wi da doin o'er time." Lessa was laughing heartily now.

"Please, Micha, let us converse in the language of the high-born. It'll be much easier for me to understand."

"Agreed," he smiled.

"You have seen much, my young friend, too much for a boy of sixteen."

"Yes, but not so bad for a man of eighteen. I'm told it has been eighteen years since the time of my birth."

"You're going to milk that, aren't you?"

"At least until I'm thirty. Lessa, I think I saw a ship coming in last night. Perhaps it could be our way off world?"

"You're determined to come with me."

"I am."

"I'd prefer you wait the three days then go back to the farm. As High Priestess I command you to do so."

"You can't command me, I'm not Borelian."

"Yes you are, there's your mark for all to see."

"Very well, I guess I have my orders. I'll just clean these utensils in the stream over there while you douse the fire. We should be on our way."

"You intend to disobey me? I could blast you to oblivion for that."

"You'd never harm a friend, Lessa, and we are friends; you said so yourself."

"Micha..."

"The ship came down that way..."

Lessa sighed and rose to her feet. "Let's be about the task then." She realized there was no way to prevent him short of killing him. Still, she feared her task would likely be harder now that she had Micha to protect.

IT WAS LATE AFTERNOON the second day before they found the ship. They soon discovered it belonged to slave raiders who were rounding up local farm women and shooting the men. They were on a slight rise, lying in the tall grass, Micha gazing through the field glasses Murtah had given him.

"I see eighteen captives and four mercs."

Lessa had her eyes closed and was breathing deeply. "Yes, eighteen captives and four mercs. There are three more crew members on the ship that you cannot see."

"The ship isn't that big, Lessa. Can we fly it ourselves?"

"We can."

"So we have no use for the mercs?"

"We do not. Why do you ask?"

"I'll go in after darkness falls."

"We'll go in after darkness falls, Micha. We'll disarm the guards and free the women. The farmers left alive will see to the fate of these men."

"Understood."

"Micha, there is something I must do; I ask for your complete trust."

"You have it, always. What are you going to do?"

"I'm going to take a great risk, and I'm going to trust in you. It would take years of training for you to develop the skills of a master of personal combat. I cannot give you the skills, but I can give you the physical attributes of such a man. Your senses will be keener, your strength greater, and your movements faster. The rest you must gain on your own. Micha, I trust in your goodness to use this gift wisely."

"I will never misuse the gifts you give me, Lessa, this I swear."

"I accept your oath," Lessa smiled at him. "Close your eyes now, and breathe deeply." As he did so, Lessa held his face in her hands and began a soft chant. Micha felt a tingling all over, and several of his muscles began to twitch for a moment. He felt the burning as a new tattoo was etched into his neck, and he smiled.

At length she sighed and pulled her hands away. Micha opened his eyes and, smiling with delight, began testing his new muscles. "Go back out of sight of the ship and practice until you've gained some control of your new body."

Grinning with delight, he scampered back down the hill. Lessa watched as he began to work through the exercises and drills that Murtah had taught him. He fell a few times at first, but soon began to move with confidence and speed.

"What have I done?" she wondered as she watched him moving faster and faster until his movements were too fast to follow. She went down the hill and stopped him. "We need to rest. You'll need some of that energy tonight."

Micha grinned and dropped to the ground beside her. He was barely breathing hard.

"I would prefer there be no killing, Micha."

"Understood."

"But?"

"It'll be more difficult, and place the women in greater danger."

"I suppose you're correct in this. They've murdered many times over, and we've witnessed some of that this day. Very well, Micha, I leave it up to you. I want you to understand that taking a man's life is a hard thing, and it will mark you."

"I know. This will not be the first time I have taken a life."

"Micha?"

"There was a guard blocking our escape from the farm when my family was killed. I took him from behind; he never knew I was there. I bashed his head in with a stone; it bothered me for many days."

Lessa nodded in understanding. "We rest then, until nightfall."

They approached silently from the dark side of the ship. Micha would create a diversion so she could slip inside and gain control. The slavers were herding the captives into the cargo hold, but the women were resisting. One young woman put up a fight. She screamed and fought as she was dragged toward the ship by the hair. Suddenly Micha appeared in the slaver's path.

"That's my girl and you can't have her. Let her go and I might let you live."

"Out of the way, boy, or I'll cut you a new one. Get your ass in there with the rest of them. A boy like you might attract a few bidders."

In response, Micha kicked him in the crotch and then twisted his grip free of the young woman's hair. He put the girl behind him and faced the angry man. The commotion caught the eye of the other three men, and they didn't see Lessa slip onto the ship. That would soon be their undoing.

The first man she encountered opened his mouth to shout, but she blew a powder into his face. He inhaled, tried to cough, then went blank. He stood there, no real life shining in his eyes at all.

"Go down to the cargo hold and await me there."

Without a sound he moved past her and proceeded to the cargo bay where he stood waiting. He was soon joined by another. As Lessa stepped onto the bridge, the man at the helm spun around. It was Mortan. "You!" he reached for his weapon but was far too slow.

"Yes me, slaver! Once again we meet, and I foil your despicable plans."

Soon he too was in the cargo hold with the others, awaiting Lessa's next command. She searched the rest of the ship but found no more men. Hurrying back to the cargo hold, she worried about how Micha was doing. She arrived just in time.

As Lessa slipped onto the ship, Micha was facing an angry mercenary. "I'll kill you for that and take your girl for myself." He lunged at Micha but grabbed only air. Micha neatly danced aside and kicked the back of the man's knee, sending him sprawling at the girl's feet. He put his boot on the back of the man's neck and pressed a weapon against his head.

"You'll apologize to my girl right now, or I'll have to blow your head off."

A hand grabbed at his collar, but he ducked away, turning as he did and discharged the weapon. His new attacker was blown meters away where he lay dead.

The last two men were coming at him now, but he kept his body between them and the young woman. He was motioning for her to back up, but she didn't. A quick glance showed her with a knife at the downed man's throat. She'd taken it from his boot. Micha grinned and winked at her, then turned back to the last two opponents.

They approached at a run, but he dove to the ground, rolling between them then striking at their hamstrings as they passed. Both men stumbled, but neither fell. They turned to face him, slowly circling around, watching for an opening, but found none. Finally both stepped back and drew energy blasters.

"So, now what are you going to do, you little shit?"

"I think I'll ask her to shoot you in the back."

"Her?"

"Yes, my friend with the blaster who is standing right behind you."

"Sure, kid." The man raised his gun, but a blast from Lessa's weapon drove him face first into the dirt. He twitched once then did not move again. His partner spun around, his gun coming up as he did. A blast from Micha's weapon blew him into the side of the ship, killing him instantly.

Micha turned to see the girl drop the bloody knife to the ground. The man who had abused her was lying in a pool of his own blood; he would not move again. She didn't speak, just gazed at him with those big brown eyes.

He was completely mesmerized until Lessa called out to him. "Micha."

"Is the ship secure, Lessa?"

"A moment," Lessa turned and spoke to the slavers she had mesmerized. "Come out now and stand over there by that dead man." She turned again to their former captives. "These are the last of the men who attacked your farms and killed your people. Take up their weapons and do with them as you will. Micha?"

He was still lost in the girl's eyes. Finally she spoke to him, "So, I'm your girl, am I?"

"Aren't you?" Micha grinned.

"I might be, but you're leaving," she said as she blushed.

"I will return." His voice was serious now. He wondered what had gotten into him?

"Micha," Lessa called again.

"Edie, my name is Edie," the girl stammered, then suddenly kissed him full on the lips.

"I'm Micha. I will return for you, Edie." With that he turned and leaped up the ramp into the belly of the ship.

"You promise?" she called from below, as the huge door began to rise.

"I swear it." He waved his reply as the door closed and hid her from his view.

"Are you sure you don't want to stay?" Lessa asked him.

"You can't fly the ship alone. We could bring her with us," Micha replied.

"Then I'd still be trying to fly the ship alone."

Micha blushed to his roots and looked away. Lessa chuckled and headed for the bridge, he followed close behind after making sure the air lock was closed. "So, where are we going, Lessa."

"The one place I would rather not be."

"And that is..."

"Borealis Prime."

"All right," Micha breathed softly as he sank into the helmsman's chair. "Borealis Prime. That should be interesting"

Three weeks later they were deep in Borelian space, and Lessa had lost count of how many times Micha had recounted the story of how Edie had protected his back during the fight with the slavers. She could recite it herself now if she chose, for he recounted it daily. Clearly her young friend was besotted with the girl.

The aging freighter wasn't challenged until they approached Borealis Prime. As they neared the planet, a warship approached. "Xoran freighter, what is your destination and business here?"

"Hello there," responded Micha. "I'm on my way to Borealis Prime to deliver a passenger."

"Who is the passenger, and what is his business here?"

"My passenger would prefer to remain anonymous. Her business is her own; I did not ask it."

"Smart mouthed pup! Prepare to be boarded and have your ship confiscated." The screen went dead and there was the sound of grapplers on the hull. The ship lurched as it was drawn close to the warship and the hatches sealed.

"All right, Lessa, I think we have company coming."

"You know what to do, Micha."

"Right, letting them in, now!" He flipped a switch and there was a hiss as the air lock opened. A full troop of soldiers stormed through the lock, arms at the ready. "I'm on the bridge with my passenger," Micha announced over the speaker. "No one else is on board."

Several of the men spread out to search the ship but found nothing. Eventually they arrived at the bridge and stormed in, weapons pointing at Lessa and Micha. "Now then, my smart mouthed young lad, let's try this again. Who are you?"

"I'm Micha, friend of Lessa, Nara clan." Micha pulled aside his collar to show his tattoos.

"Where did you get that mark, boy?"

He grabbed Micha by the shirt and hauled him to his feet, but gulped as he felt the point of the blade against his throat. "Don't wrinkle the shirt; I hate that. Now, step back and be polite. Ask me again."

He swallowed hard then stepped quickly back as Micha sheathed the knife. "Where did you get that mark?" He was more polite this time.

"I gave it to him." The rich contralto voice came from the graceful figure standing near the vid screen. As they turned to that voice, Lessa pulled aside her scarf to show her tattoos. Every man lowered his weapons and sank to one knee.

"Lady Arlessa! Praised is this day. You have returned to us. Praised be the day."

"Stop babbling and rise. Listen carefully. I want my return to be a surprise, and without fanfare. You will take the following commands to your captain. Make no communication, but your ship will escort my own to the temple. Do you understand your orders?"

"Understood, Lady." He leaped to his feet and led his troops back to the air lock and into their own ship. There was a hiss as the lock closed and the life tunnel from the big ship withdrew. A moment later there was a squawk on the communicator.

"Freighter, this is Captain Darnak of the Long Blade, Raptor Class Battle Cruiser. This is a secure channel. Is there any truth to this madman's tale, or did you give him a sample of the intoxicants you're smuggling?"

Lessa stepped in front of the vid screen so the captain could see her. He gasped and dropped to one knee. "Stand captain. You received my instructions?"

"Yes, Lady. The controllers will ask, but I shall tell them I'm escorting the freighter in on temple business. That will stop their questions. Lady, welcome home."

"Thank you, Captain. Arlessa out." She broke the connection and sighed. "Well, the cat's out of the bag now."

"Do you think we'll have time?"

"All I need to do is find that library, and then we'll have all the time we need. We simply have to avoid capture."

"Capture? Aren't you the high priestess? Don't you command there?" "A high priestess commands until she is married off to the Viceroy, another trophy for his harem. An inhibitor is placed at the base of her brain to keep her compliant. It's a fate worse than death, Micha, and one I escaped. It's the Lady Regent who would truly command then. I expect them to make a show, but to try to capture us, plant the inhibitor on me, and then hand me over to the Viceroy."

Micha's posture stiffened. "I won't let that happen, Lessa. I swear it."

Learning to Survive

B renna sat staring at her hands, not making a sound. She had hardly
moved for days.

"Brenna, will you not eat?"

"I'm not hungry, Ena, thank you."

Ena came and sat beside her. "She wouldn't want this from you,
Brenna O'Loran. You know this to be true."

"I know. Ena, it's all so strange. I was always so self-sufficient and
self-assured, now look at me. I can't seem to function without her. Odd,
I was never attracted to women before, but the moment I looked into
her eyes, I lost myself. I struggled for words, I lost track of what I was
doing; tell me truly, did she bewitch me?"

"Oh yes," laughed Ena, "she bewitched you alright, but not in the
way you think. You're love struck and besotted, my dear. It happens to
the best of us." She paused a moment then spoke again. "In truth, this
time of separation is a gift to you."

"A gift, what do you mean, a gift?"

"You've been under the spell of the Novan Witch for months now.
It's time for you to regain your sense of self, your strength of purpose.
Once you've regained yourself, you can be a much better partner for
her. She's a powerful witch, and quite strong willed. You'll need to be
strong and resourceful, for I believe you're in for an exciting life."

"Perhaps you're right, Ena. Do you truly believe she will return?"

"Oh yes, it's only a question of when. Remember Brenna, she can
time shift. Lessa will do what she has set herself to do and then she'll
return. I expect to see her soon, but as an older, wiser, stronger woman
than she was when she left two days ago. She may experience years in
the time she's gone. You'll need to grow strong swiftly to be ready."

"How do you know this, Ena, and how can you tell when someone speaks true or not?"

Ena laughed heartily. "I thought you might have guessed by now. I was young, training at the temple on Borealis Three, when I fell in love with a giant warrior. Our love was forbidden, as I had already been promised to a nobleman.

"We were discovered, and I was sent to the slave quarters, my warrior was falsely accused, then imprisoned. I slipped away in the night and set him free. We fled, and after years on the run, we ended up at this place."

"So, you're witch-trained too?"

"Some, but I had no real talent for it. I'm much happier here."

"You're right. I can't sit here moping like a spoiled child. There's much work to be done and I must be about the things I do best. Is there a place I can use as a school for the children?"

"The eating hall is free during the day. Brenna, would you consider teaching our children as well?" "Of course! Any school must be for all children. After the clean-up from the evening meal, I will also teach any adults who wish to learn."

It began the next day. Brenna rose early to help with the morning meal and clean up. She then helped all the children finish their chores before calling them in to lessons. She had no histories or other teaching aids, so she taught what she could from memory. She did the same at night for some of the adults.

Brenna also taught high born speech patterns as well as noble manners and taught them to read. These would be useful skills should they ever leave this world.

It wasn't all teaching for Brenna O'Loran though. She also became a student. By helping the children, she learned survival skills honed through life on a rough planet. These were good skills to have. She also convinced Murtah to teach combat training to everybody, including the women and children. If slavers should ever come to this farm commune, they would not find easy prey.

About three weeks after Lessa's departure, a stranger approached. A young woman, a girl really, with ragged clothes, wandered up to the farm. She was tired, hungry, and dehydrated. They brought her to the school and gave her to Brenna. Food and water were swiftly set before her.

Lessons stopped while she ate, for they all wanted to hear her story. Brenna convinced her to save it until the evening meal so all could hear. Later that evening as the meal ended and everyone relaxed with full bellies, the girl was called upon to tell her story. She rose to her feet and, blushing at all the attention, began her tale.

"My name is Edie; I seek the farm from which Micha came."

"What do you know of Micha?" asked Brenna. "Was he alone when you saw him?"

"He was well and had a companion, a tall woman with light hair who seemed to be in command. The slavers came and killed the men and older women of our farm. The rest of us were taken to their spaceship. We were to be taken to Dornal Three and sold as slaves.

One of them grabbed my hair and dragged me toward the ship. That's when Micha appeared. He claimed me as his own and fought for me. Four men he fought and defeated."

"He claimed you?" remarked Murtah. "Micha is a bit young to be claiming a mate. You accepted his claim?"

"I did. You should have seen him. He had no fear of those men, even though they had killed many. Micha may be young, but there is no other man I know of who could have defended me against the slavers. I just hope he can farm."

There was a great round of laughter at that. "Micha is the best farmer of us all, Edie. Tell us more."

"There is little more to tell. He claimed me and swore to return for me, and then they flew away in the slaver's ship."

"The slavers?"

"Four dead and three working as labor slaves to repair the damage they did."

"So, why did you come here, Edie?" asked Brenna.

"The farm where I was taken is some distance from the ship where he claimed me. He wouldn't know where to look for me, so I thought I should find his farm and be waiting for him at the time of his return. I went to every farm I could find, and was about to give up, when a man told me of the place where most men no longer wanted to go.

They said there was once a farm there, so I took a chance and here I am. I'm strong and will work hard. I've been claimed by one of your own, will you take me in?"

"You're welcome here, Edie," smiled Murtah. "Miss O'Loran will see to you. I believe she could use an assistant."

"Will you accept me?" she asked as she turned to Brenna.

"Yes, Edie, I will accept you. The tall woman with Micha was my mate. We'll await their return together."

"Edie, do your parents know where you have gone?" asked Ena, as she approached.

"All are dead," replied the girl, as the tears suddenly rose up and overtook her.

Ena folded the girl into her arms and rocked her gently. "Then since one of our own has claimed you, we're now your family. This is now your home." There was a murmur of agreement.

Later that night, as Ena cuddled onto Murtah's shoulder, she sighed deeply then spoke. "Murtah, do you think Micha is too young. For that matter, do you think he was serious?"

"I believe he was, my love. The girl told the truth of the tale, for you would know if she lied. Micha may be young in years, but there is an old soul behind those eyes. He will return for the girl if he is able. If he doesn't, we shall regard her as a widow and treat her accordingly."

"He's with the high priestess, Murtah, the strongest witch in nine generations. The girl won't be widowed any time soon."

As time passed, it was Edie who managed to get Alla to speak. It was only a few syllables at first, but after a while they were chattering away like sisters. Edie wanted to know everything about Micha and Alla, like any younger sister, was all too willing to share.

Returned

There was a great deal of commotion and excitement as the old freighter sank slowly toward the temple's private landing pad. That pad was reserved for the high priestess, and had not been in use for years. Word spread like wildfire that she was returning.

Many thrilled to the news, but others were incensed. The Lady Regent, Salian, strode regally toward the ship, outrage clear on her face. The great warship that had remained above the freighter rose and returned to space as she appeared.

The crackling communicators that had ordered the two ships away had been ignored. Salian, dressed in the full flowing robes of her office, stood glaring and gathering her strength. Whatever the Viceroy's minions were up to this time would be thwarted right here. The temple would not be forced, coerced, or manipulated into declaring a new high priestess.

Arlessa was still alive. The temple would have known if she had perished. As the cargo ramp began to descend, Salian spoke in a clear ringing voice, highly enhanced by her power. "Be gone from this sacred place, defiler, or face the consequences of your foolish actions."

To her astonishment, a young man in a baggy uniform walked out of the ship. He smiled at her and she sent a wave of power at him, designed to put him on his backside. It had no effect at all. Salian felt the strength of the power that opposed her, and she knew Arlessa had returned. No one else alive could have stopped her so easily.

The young man walked up to her then dropped to one knee. "Greetings, great Lady of the Temple, I bring a passenger who would speak with you in private. She asks that you join her aboard the ship."

"Who is your passenger, boy?"

"I'm Micha, friend of Lessa, son of Kona, Nara Clan."

"I asked the name of your passenger. Stop being impertinent and answer me at once."

"You know full well who his passenger is, Salian." Lessa's stern voice preceded her appearance. To all eyes but Micha's, she was dressed in the full robes of her office. He still saw her ragged uniform.

"Looks like we may need a backup plan after all," he muttered under his breath.

"Since you would not speak in private, Salian, we will do things your way. Go, have our chambers prepared, and call an assembly in the Hall of Audience."

"You cannot just walk back in here after all these years and start throwing orders around, Arlessa. I rule here now. Your authority has been removed by the council."

"The council? You mean the minions of the Viceroy. Does that include you Salian? No? I thought not. You want to keep the mantle of power for yourself." Lessa had a cold smile on her face. "Push me, Salian, and you will discover the true reach of my abilities. Now obey me."

Face contorting with rage, Salian bowed and withdrew. She knew most of the temple's inhabitants had witnessed her defeat. Arlessa had changed much in the years of her absence. This woman was no figurehead high priestess bound for the Viceroy's harem; she was a full Novan witch, the first in generations. Provoked she could reduce the temple to rubble before they could get her under control, if they ever could.

Motioning for Micha to follow, Lessa strode into the temple as though she owned the place. The crowd of people parted before her as she made her way inside. She led him through a maze of corridors, moving ever deeper into the temple. She smiled slightly as she saw his lips moving. Micha was memorizing the turns they had taken. If things went awry, he would know the way out. Finally she slowed, lightly drawing her fingers along the wall as though searching for a hidden door. She found none.

Cursing softly, she searched the wall again. Still nothing! "Guard me, Micha, I must focus." He spun easily, his back to her and a blaster in each hand. No one would disturb her.

Lessa closed her eyes and concentrated. After a long moment she sighed and opened them. "It's gone. They've moved the library. I didn't want to have to do it this way. Ah well, it cannot be helped. Our task will take a bit longer, Micha."

"I'll watch, Lessa. Do what you need to do; you won't be disturbed."

She sank to the floor, sitting in a cross legged position, and began breathing deeply. As her focus shifted to other worlds, Micha's eyes roved from one opening to another along the corridor. From time to time a face would appear at the end of the passageway, but his raised blaster sent them scurrying away.

Finally, a group of three priestesses approached. One waved her hand and his blaster went flying down the hall. Micha put away the other blaster away and approached them. "Do not disturb her. I have no wish to harm anyone, but she must not be disturbed."

"You threaten me child, how dare you?" The woman's voice was too loud, and before the words died on the air he was behind her with a blade at her throat. She gulped and didn't move.

"Be silent now," he whispered. "I have no wish to harm you, but the high priestess must not be disturbed."

"Your death will be slow and painful," hissed one of the others. "How dare you threaten a priestess of the temple?"

"I'm the guardian of High Priestess Arlessa. She gave instruction not to be disturbed."

"She won't find it, boy, for it's gone. She'll never find it again. You're throwing your life away for nothing!"

"Unless you want this one's blood on the floor, you will be quiet. I'd also be wary of annoying the high priestess. Terrible things happen when she is annoyed. Kneel before her now and be silent."

A few moments later, Lessa's eyes popped open, and she rose gracefully to her feet. She was frustrated and letting it show. Spotting his blaster down the hall she thrust her hand toward it. The blaster leaped from the floor and sailed to her waiting hand. She returned it to Micha who spun it easily back into its holster.

"What has happened here?"

"Lady, these three approached and begged an audience. They've been very patient."

"So I see. What do you want?"

"You'll never find it, Arlessa. It's been destroyed."

"Micha, cut the tongue from the next one who lies to me."

"As you desire, Lady, so shall it be done." He was grinning now and fingering the blade.

"Neither of you nor all of you combined, have the power to destroy it. Where is it?"

"I don't know, the regent and the elder council tried to destroy it but could not. They hid it so none would ever find it again. No one should ever be able to use that dark power, not even you, Arlessa."

"Hidden? Very well. Has the assembly been called?"

"Yes."

"Why are you not there?"

"We go, Lady." They leaped to their feet and scurried away.

"Micha?"

"No one was harmed, Lessa, I used threats only. That one was strong, though," as he pointed toward the tallest of the three priestesses. "Thank you for the enhancements you gave me."

"Come Micha. We go to the assembly. I sense treachery afoot."

"As do I, Lessa. Let me lead the way. If there's a trap you may be able to escape."

"Micha…"

"If they capture you, I won't be able to help you. If I'm captured, you can still find the library then come back for me."

"All right, you win, but you don't have to be so smug," Lessa smiled warmly at her loyal friend.

"I love winning," he grinned. "Point the way."

They wound their way through several twisting corridors until they finally reached the central assembly hall; a gathered crowd of people was waiting for them. A young girl's eyes gave it away as they stepped through the archway. She glanced upwards. The enchanted nets were still in the air when Micha spun and thrust Lessa back. "Run."

The nets fell on him, pinning him to the floor. "Run, Lessa." She closed her eyes, took a step forward, and vanished. Micha was wrapped up in the nets and stood on his feet. He was unable to move a muscle. "Where is she?" The woman snarling in his face was the one he had put his blade to.

He grinned at her. "Now you've made the high priestess angry. You won't like her when she's angry."

"Pah, take him to the cells. A week of torture will loosen his tongue."

"Torture is a waste of time," Salian sighed. "He cannot tell what he doesn't know. One as young as he is wouldn't be privy to a priestess's plans. Throw him in the cells. We'll deal with him later."

Searching

As Micha pushed her back Lessa knew it was too late. She couldn't help him, and she couldn't help herself if she was captured. She closed her eyes and stepped through the doorway of time. Another step and she was back in the assembly hall, it was empty now. A glance at the wall chronometer told her a week had passed.

Ducking into a side corridor, Lessa quickly found the hidden tunnel she had discovered as a child. A short while later she was behind the tapestry in the offices of the high priestess, which Salian was now using as her own. She smiled as she listened.

"There's no sign of her, Regent," sighed the old priestess. "We've searched the entire temple from top to bottom several times over the past week, and there's been no sign of her. Perhaps we should torture that servant of hers."

"Sadly, that's no longer an option, at least until we catch him again."

"Catch him again?"

"He escaped. I have no idea how. Since the middle of the first night several of the cells have been empty."

"Several cells?"

"He took several criminals and a couple of untrained slaves with him. The gods alone know where he's gone."

"Perhaps she took him."

"Perhaps she did. No matter, they'll never find the black witch's library. That spell was cast by the five women on the council the day they found her in it. Only one of the five can break it, and Merilla is the only one left alive."

"How is Merilla these days?"

"Failing fast, her mind is nearly gone. She's confined to a bed in the infirmary now, tended day and night. The slaves say she just babbles incoherently."

Lessa didn't stay to hear more, but silently slipped away, heading for the infirmary. It was midday. She would have to wait until late at night. Lessa hid herself in a storage closet and sank to the floor to sleep. Sleeping anywhere anytime is an old soldier's trick and she had learned it long ago on the battlefields.

When she awakened and peeked through the keyhole, all was in semi darkness. Dim lighting allowed the three attendants to walk among the beds and tend the sleeping patients. Lessa smiled. The shadows would be her friend.

She chanted softly for a moment or two and then looked again. All the attendants were asleep. Lessa slipped from her hiding place and entered the infirmary. Softly she went from bed to bed until she found the old woman. Gently she laid her hand on the woman's forehead and sent a small rush of healing energy. The old woman opened her eyes.

She did not recognize Lessa, she just began to mumble incoherently, or so it would have seemed to most, but Lessa grinned. This was the language of the woman's birth planet. Daughter of a slave, she had first learned the speech of the farmers. This was a language Micha had taught Lessa on the trip, as a way to pass the time and fight the boredom of a long space flight.

It took mere moments for Lessa to gently guide the old woman's wandering thoughts. She first learned the spell that was used to hide the library, then the chant to break it. Only then did she seek the location. So that was why she couldn't find it! The library was no longer on this planet.

It was time to find Micha and get out of there.

AS THE TEMPLE GUARDS had dragged him off to the prison cells in the lower levels of the complex, Micha wondered why a temple would even need a prison. He'd been stripped of his weapons and tossed unceremoniously into a cell. As the door slammed shut behind him, he shouted, "This is a poor way to treat the personal guard of a high priestess!"

His captors laughed as they walked away. Good, they were gone. Micha stood and began a slow and detailed inspection of his cell.

"You're wasting your time," said a deep voice from the next cell. "I've been here for over two years and can't find a way out. The damned place is enchanted."

"I'm sure it is. You don't mind if I try, do you? I don't seem to have an entertainment screen in my cell."

"Suit yourself," chuckled the deep voice. "Who are you, my young friend?"

"I'm Micha, friend of Lessa, personal guard of the High Priestess, Nara Clan."

"Of course you are, boy. I must have been here longer than I thought for I don't recognize your name. I'm Nara Clan. Who is your father?"

"He's dead," replied Micha as he continued his inspection, "but, I was combat trained by Murtah."

"Ha, you lie, boy, Murtah is dead. I know for he's my brother."

"Oh he's far from dead. I left his farm less than a month ago. Listen, we're both Nara Clan, so we must help each other. We'll leave this place together. Eventually we'll return to Murtah's farm."

"Are you telling the truth, boy? Is my brother really alive?"

"He is. Can you see through the cracks enough to recognize my tattoos?"

"I can. Who are you, Micha? You look to be about sixteen, yet you have a combat master's mark."

"I told you, I'm personal guard of Arlessa, High Priestess of the Temple. It was she who gave me both marks."

"Damned if I don't believe you! But it matters not, we can't escape. It's enough to know that Murtah has survived. You said Arlessa had returned. If that's true, why are you here in prison?"

"It wasn't a warm reception. Tell me, when do they feed us?"

"Hungry already?" chuckled the deep voice.

"How many come to bring the meals?"

"Only two, one slave and one guard."

"Let me know in advance so I can be hiding behind the door when they arrive."

"That sounds like a good idea. How do you plan to get out of that cell?"

"I'm already out of the cell, now I'm looking for something I can use for a weapon."

There was a crash as the big man hurled himself against the door of his cell, the bars of the small window clenched in his fists. He was looking out at a smiling Micha. "How?"

"I have a full door of bars, they're enchanted, but it's easy enough to wriggle between them if you have the knack. I'm Micha." He stuck his hand through the bars and the big man shook it.

"I'm Zartah, brother of Murtah. Well met, clansman. What next?"

"Next I find a weapon or do without one, but when they bring the food I'll get the keys and let you out, all of you. Where we go from there, I don't know."

"If there's a way out of here, it'll be through the catacombs. Even the witches are afraid to go down there. If we try to go up they'll just bewitch us and bring us back."

"Excellent! We have a plan. Now, what'll we do for a back-up plan?"

"Back-up plan?"

"Always have a back-up plan, Zartah," grinned Micha.

There was nothing to use as a weapon, so Micha simply sat down and waited. It was a long while before he heard the noisy approach of the guard and slave. As they entered, Zartah was making a fuss to hold their attention. Micha kicked the back of the slave's leg and as he fell forward, Micha grabbed the tray from his hand and smacked the guard with it.

The man fell to the floor, unconscious. The slave rolled quickly away and put his back to the wall. Micha put his finger to his lips for silence as he fished the keys from the guard's belt. The slave made no sound.

Micha swiftly released Zartah and installed the guard in the cell. He then released all the prisoners. A few moments later they were slipping down a seemingly endless staircase, going ever deeper under the temple, taking the slave and several more of their fellow prisoners with them. At last they reached the bottom.

Groping around, Zartah found a torch and flint tied to a string. He tried to get the torch going, but failed until Micha produced a lighter stick so he could see what he was doing. "Where did you get that?"

"Over here, there's a bunch of them." Zartah snorted as he cast aside the flint.

"Damned ancient technology, ah, there we are. Now, let's see what we can find down here."

They made their way slowly, ever mindful of possible traps. The place seemed to be an endless maze of crypts, heavy with dust, and few signs of life except a rodent or two. The group was becoming restless when finally the light showed a way out: a twisted, half collapsed tunnel that led upwards.

They were well into the tunnel when the torch died, leaving them in darkness. There were some whimpers of fear, but Zartah's deep booming voice brought order.

"Join hands with the man in front of you, said Micha. "We have to stay together. No one gets left behind."

There was a shuffling and grunting, but the line of people, seven men and four women, plus Micha, moved forward again. A short while later they found themselves in a cavern with light filtering down from above. The former prison slave began to babble, but Micha stopped him. He spoke to him in 'farm-speak' for a moment and then sighed.

"It seems we're just outside the temple, but he's afraid to go farther. He says that if we go into the city he'll be sent back to the temple and tortured."

"We'll all be tortured to death once they catch us," breathed another.

"Then we'd better make sure they don't catch us," said a third. "My name's Gorda. I have friends in the city; they can help us."

"Can they get us transport north?" asked Zartah.

"I expect so."

"We should wait until darkness falls," said Micha. "Everyone rest as best they can."

"Why did you help us, young one?" asked one of the escapees.

"Yes, you and he are clan, but most of us aren't, why help us?" asked one of the women.

"You're Kella, yes? Someone once helped me when I needed it most. Perhaps one day you can do the same for another." Micha smiled once more before settling down to sleep.

LESSA SILENTLY SCANNED the temple, but Micha was nowhere to be found. She sent her awareness deeper, into the catacombs. Micha had been there, but that was several days past. Lessa's frustration grew. She didn't have a lot of time for this, and Salian's temple-trained underlings would know she was searching. They would sense it and then find her.

Letting herself into one of the temple's vast storerooms, Lessa quickly dressed herself as a supplicant of the middle class. As the sun set, she slipped out of the complex and joined a group of people taking the mass transit back into the city. No one recognized her as she left the temple.

Locating a small rooming house, Lessa settled in for the night. Sitting cross legged on the floor, she sent her awareness out in search of Micha. Maybe he had managed to reach the city. Finally, she found his trail, but it was days old. He'd gone north on private transport.

Lessa smiled. Her resourceful young friend must have made an ally somewhere and was now on his way to the homeland of Nara Clan. Very well, that would be where she would look for him. Next morning she headed north.

———◉———

TWO DAYS LATER LESSA found Micha in a small dingy pub on the wrong side of Genoa city, the seat of the Nara Clan's government. A few unruly patrons gave her the once over as she entered, but Micha and a tall man were at her side in a moment, she'd known she was coming. The tall man started to kneel, but Micha kicked his shin and stopped him.

"Come this way, Lessa. Everyone else is already here."

Micha led her to a corner where several men and women were gathered. He introduced her to each in turn then passed her a mug of poor wine. She passed her hand over it and the wine glowed momentarily. Taking a sip, Lessa sighed appreciatively.

"You must be kin to Murtah," she said turning to Zartah.

"He's my brother, Lady," he replied. "Micha says he's alive and well."

"He was when last we saw him. I believe he still is, for it was a peaceful place."

"Did you find what you were looking for, Lessa?"

"No, but I learned its location. We'll need a ship, for it's no longer on this planet." +

"Where is it, Lessa?"

"Kuris Morn."

"Alas, whatever it is you seek is now beyond your reach, Lady. Kuris Morn is Arlen Alliance territory now. Most of the planet was destroyed in the war, for the fighting there was fierce."

"That which I seek cannot be destroyed, Zartah. "I care not who holds title to the planet, I must go there, and swiftly."

"It'll be good to visit the home world again," grinned Micha.

"Better you should stay here among friends, Micha."

"You'll only get into trouble if I let you go alone, Lessa. Besides, I speak the language."

"He's right, Lady. If you know the location, let us bring a few men and a small fighter ship. Gorda here is a specialist," said Zartah, gesturing to the man on his left.

"Mercenary?"

"Yes, Lady, I have years of experience as well, and I owe young Micha my life. I can get three more good men and a fighter ship. We'll need a freighter to get us close to Kuris Morn, but we can shoot in from behind the nearby moon and reach the ground swiftly. A small ship coming in fast at full burn will look like a meteor burning up in the atmosphere to their sensors."

"Lady, we could approach Lortax, clan chieftain now, for help," suggested Zartah. "He might go to war for you, but it would take more than just Nara clan to dislodge the Arlens from Kuris Morn."

Lessa shook her head. "No, Zartah, I dare not ask the Chieftain for help, even though we were childhood friends. The Viceroy would learn of it too quickly and the clan could suffer needlessly." She turned back to Gorda. "All right, if you're determined to take this course, I'd be grateful for the assistance."

"There are rooms here, such as they are, Lady. Take your ease here tonight and I'll come for you in the morning." Gorda was on his feet and gone in a heartbeat.

"We should all get some rest," said Micha. "Lady, I'll escort you to your room." The room was spare, but Lessa was grateful for the chance to rest. As she lay on the tiny bed, her mind wandered back to Brenna and the others. The separation was harder than she expected. She missed Brenna's company, the sound of her voice and the scent of her hair.

Lessa sighed aloud, in spite of herself. She closed her eyes and focused her thoughts on her lover, letting her affection and regard flow freely from her heart, like a glistening silver thread, bridging the space between them.

In her mind's eye, Brenna's face emerged. Lessa's breathing deepened and her astral body rose from the small bed, travelling the thread across space and time, arriving in Brenna's darkened room. Her beloved was sleeping. Another woman shared the room and Lessa wondered who it might be.

The woman rolled in her sleep and Lessa smiled as she recognized Micha's chosen. Lessa stood there a while listening to Brenna breathe and watching her breasts gently rise and fall. How she loved this woman!

She leaned over Brenna's slumbering form and lightly kissed her lips. Brenna's nose wrinkled and then she smiled in her sleep. Lessa's heart tightened. "I will return to you, my love," she whispered before finding her way back to her own body.

Content that her beloved was well, Lessa slept dreamlessly for several hours. Gorda returned for them at first light. Taking a paid transport, they soon arrived at the space port freight yards. The freighter he'd somehow managed to acquire was small. Gorda had four hardened warriors with him, three men and a woman. Lessa, Micha, and Zartah made eight in all. The fighter ship they were carrying in the cargo hold was only designed to carry six. It was promising to be a cozy trip.

War Comes

A nother month passed uneventfully on the farm, but the time of peace was about to end. Each evening was devoted to speculation about what would happen if the witch's spell failed. The spell could work well under normal circumstances, but would it buckle under the stress of direct bombardment.

If it did, what would they do? How would they escape? The folk made plans as best they could, but they could do little except wait. One morning the children ran from the school to watch fireworks in the sky. The adults were already there.

Soon they heard the sounds of heavy land-based cannon and the scream of bombers dropping their payload. The battle was not far from the farm, for the ground shook from the impact of the bombs. War had come to Kora Six. It was time to prepare for the inevitable. Sooner or later everyone would have to leave the farm and they knew it.

Later that day, as the adults sat discussing the battle they'd seen play out overhead, a shout came from the boy who was on lookout. "Soldier coming in!" Murtah motioned for the others to remain while he went out to see what was going on. How had a soldier managed to get through the witch's spell anyway?

"Greetings, Farmer, I'm Sgt. Dek Borkin. I mean no harm, but would speak to your folk, if I may. I'll leave my weapons outside if you wish."

"Set them inside the door and come join us for a meal." Murtah took the man inside and settled him at table. Everyone waited until he had finished eating before plying him with questions.

"Hear me, good folk," Dek said as he rose to his feet to speak, "for I bring hard news indeed. The Arlen Alliance has made peace, and allied with, the Varona Guild. This new and more powerful alliance has turned its attention to the Ninth Planetary Union. The Ninth has drawn the Maccay System into its own alliance. This puts Kora Six in a position of great strategic importance. The battle for supremacy has already begun as I'm sure you noticed.

"My people, the Maccay, have been evacuating everybody they find from here to Iona Three, a small planet in our system. It has good soil for farming and a fairly small population. You will receive all the help you need to get set up again once you arrive."

"What happens if we refuse to go?" asked Edie.

"Young miss, you can't stay. Your farm is in the middle of a battlefield and will be overrun by one faction or the other. It'll be trampled down, blown up, and shot to the nine hells of Porapix. You cannot stay."

"I won't leave. My mate is off world, and I must be here when he returns," Edie exclaimed.

"As must I," declared Brenna. "My mate is off world as well, and I can't leave this place. She won't know what's become of me, or where to find me." Brenna reached out to hug Edie who was starting to cry.

"Please, you're good and generous people. We would not see you harmed or enslaved. Please reconsider."

"Why are you so concerned for us?" asked Murtah cautiously.

Dek grinned as he replied. "I do have an ulterior motive, I readily admit. One of our main agricultural planets, Uras Ten, was laid waste in the last battles with the Arlens six years ago. We haven't been able to replace those agri-supplies and many of our people go hungry each night.

Maccay is desperate for good farmers. We would re-locate you there and set you up with more modern machinery, better growing soil, and climate, as well as ready markets for your harvest. As for this place, it'll probably be used as a hospital area for the wounded."

"Are we to have no say in this at all?" Ena asked impatiently.

"Think, Ena," Murtah sighed. "We'll get no such generosity from the Arlens, and well you know it."

"I see many of you folk are Borealans," said Dek. "We could send you home if you wish."

"That won't be necessary," Murtah chuckled. "My people, war is upon us and we're too few to defend this homeland. I suggest we take this man's offer. It's better to start over in another place than to die defending what's already lost. We always knew this day could come, but fate has dealt us another hand of cards. I say we go."

There was a full agreement, except for Brenna and Edie. "You'll need people to care for the wounded if you turn this into a hospital area," sighed Brenna. "I'll stay to nurse the wounded."

"As will I." agreed Edie.

"Then we will all stay," said Ena. "We won't leave you two behind."

"Go, Ena, dear friend." Brenna laid her hand lightly on the older woman's shoulder. "Take the children and keep them safe for me. As soon as Lessa and Micha return we'll join you on Iona Three."

The discussion continued a while, but in the end, Brenna and Edie were adamant and would not be swayed. The soldier promised Murtah that the Maccay would watch out for them, so the farmers agreed to go.

The next morning, the people of the farm began the long trek to the Maccay transport that would take them to safety and a new home. As they marched away the soldier turned to Murtah. "Can you tell me why we can't bring a troop carrier here for you, and why most of our men were terrified to come to the farm?"

"Yes, I could tell you," Murtah offered, "but then I'd just have to shoot you. Maybe it is best you don't know."

"Aye, if that is the case, then it is best I don't know," Dek replied grinning. "I won't ask again. So, when did the Lady leave?"

"She left months ago and won't return."

"So, she yet lives and runs free. That's a good sign indeed. I'll leave you now. Men will meet you on that rise and guide you from there."

By noon the next day, a full field hospital had been set up at the farm. Troop carriers carrying materials and wounded were able to enter, but the armed guards were unable to pass the borders of the farm.

By the end of the week the hospital was over flowing with wounded. Brenna and Edie assisted the medics as best they could. There was no let up. Lessa's spell kept the farm safe, but by the end of the second week it too was filling up with wounded. Each night the two women dragged themselves back to their small hut and fell instantly asleep.

The pace was exhausting, but another problem was brewing for Brenna and Edie. They were the lone women in a growing company of men, and Lessa's spell was weakening. Some of the soldiers began to make unwelcomed suggestions and were getting bolder. Brenna decided to put a stop to it. She was tired of explaining that she was taken. She marched into the commander's tent and leaned her tiny fists on his desk.

He sighed as he dropped his reading tablet and leaned back in his chair. "Miss O'Loran, I know you're a high born lady, but these men are sorely wounded. They're just playing, trying to take their minds off the pain and war."

"I'm not here about that this time."

"Oh, what then?"

"You need a dispatcher and, as you have lamented many times, there are none available to come this far into the war zone."

"Yes, so?"

"Give me the kit. I'll do the job."

"Brenna, Miss O'Loran, this isn't to be taken on lightly. To take a man's life as he looks into your eyes, well, it takes a hard person to do this. It does something to you. I've seen..."

"It can be no harder than seeing them suffer and hearing them beg for death to stop the pain."

"All right, but you must swear to me you'll only do this as a last resort. If you do I'll administer the oath and give you the kit."

"I'm not a murderer, Commander, but I can no longer stand the level of suffering. We're pinned down here with more wounded coming in every hour, and our supplies are running out. It's time for a more practical approach. Someone must do this. Better it be me than one of your own."

His shoulders sagged as he yielded to her logic. "Here's the kit. There are thirty charges in here. One charge to the chest and a man will slip away peacefully. Remember, you have to look into his eyes as you do this."

"I understand, Commander." She raised her hand to her heart and repeated the oath as he gave it to her. Brenna swung the strap over her shoulder and left the tent. As she returned to the food tent she found Edie sitting at a table. The soldier leaning over her was getting far too friendly. Edie brushed away his hand, ignoring him, but her face was red with anger.

As the man's hand reached toward her shoulder once again, a small hand grasped his wrist. "Leave her alone, she's been claimed and doesn't want your attentions."

"Ah, perhaps you would prefer my touch," he grinned as he pried her fingers off his wrist, but held onto her hand.

Suddenly a crutch cracked him across the wrist. "Let her go, Lukan, you fool."

"What the hell is wrong with you, have you got a death wish?" The man battered aside the offending crutch and grabbed its owner by the collar. "I don't, but perhaps you do. Look at her kit, Lukan, look at her armband. You're going back to the front tomorrow. Next time you come in here on a stretcher, she might be making the decision for you."

"Dispatcher? Ma'am, I'm so sorry, I didn't know, I..."

"Stay away from me and my assistant." Brenna turned aside from him and sat beside Edie. She began talking about the supplies they needed for the next set of rounds and ignored the men completely. Word traveled fast that the hospital now had a dispatcher. The men were much more respectful, some were outwardly fearful and most no longer looked forward to Brenna's visits.

Nearly a week passed before they realized they could trust her to be fair. Brenna hadn't dispatched a single man lying in a bed, and only one poor soul who came in on a stretcher more dead than alive. Three days later the commander called her into his tent again. He wouldn't look her in the eye. "Brenna, I need you to empty ten beds today."

"What???" "We need ten beds. You have to make them available."

"I won't do it! The decision to dispatch or not is mine alone to make. You actually expect me to murder ten men to..."

"Brenna, you're holding back. There are men there who can't recover, not ever, yet they could linger for months using up space and resources stronger men could use to recover."

"So you can send them back out to get shot to hell all over again."

"It's the nature of war. Look, we wanted you to leave, but you wouldn't go. You then demanded to be the dispatcher. I tried to talk you out of it, but you were adamant. This task falls to you, and you have no choice but to do it."

He had finally met her eyes and she was glaring at him. "You knew this would happen but didn't tell me."

"I couldn't be certain, but since you accepted the kit and the role, you can't step aside from it now."

"Tonight then, after darkness falls," she said, her voice trembling.

"It must be done now, Brenna."

"Then you do it, for I will not!" she spat back at him.

"All right, woman, tonight, but ten beds, nothing less."

"I can count," she muttered as she stormed out of his tent and sought out the hut she shared with Edie.

Edie found her there, crying her eyes out. "Brenna, what is it?"

The girl gathered the small woman into her arms and rocked her gently. Brenna sobbed out the tale of what she would have to do. "Oh Edie, I miss Lessa so much. What am I going to do?"

"What would she tell you now?"

"She would tell me to be strong for the men I must help to the other side. She would tell me it's better for them to look into the gentle loving eyes of a woman than a hard-eyed man who has no feeling. She would tell me how men are often taken from bed and dumped out in the fields, still alive, but with no hope of recovery. She would ask me to be gentle with them and myself. Oh gods, Edie, I'd sell my soul for one touch of her hand right now."

"I know, I know, dear friend. Can I help you do this?"

"Edie?" "I can, Brenna, if I must. Better they be at peace than in pain forever."

"No, this is my task, and I must be strong and do it. If I ask another to do this for me, how could I ever look her in the eyes again? Lessa could do this Edie. She could face death and help soldiers cross over. I must be worthy of her, I must."

"Then do this as she would, Brenna. Imagine her hand on your shoulder as you go and do this as she would have it done."

"So much wisdom in one so young," sniffed Brenna as she leaned back and laid her hand on Edie's cheek. "You and Micha will make a fine pair. I'll rest now. Wake me at full darkness?"

"I will."

Several hours later Edie gently shook Brenna's shoulder. "It's time, Brenna. Do you want me to accompany you?"

"No, Edie, you rest. This is my task and I'm determined to do it."

She rose, swept up the black bag and stepped out into the dim light of the compound at night. As quietly as she could, Brenna approached and gently awakened the first man. He groaned in pain as he opened his eyes.

"So, you have come for me at last."

"I'm sorry, but your wounds are deep and have gone septic..."

"It's all right," he sighed as he lightly touched her arm. "I've been expecting you. Commander's orders?"

"Yes. I am sorry..."

"Hush now, I'm weary of the pain and ready to face the mystery." He turned to her as best he could, looking deeply into her eyes. "I'm Marden, son of Kard, I'm ready."

"I'm Brenna, mate of Lessa," she replied, her voice trembling, "I've come to ease your journey."

"Thank you, Lady."

Brenna paused as the dying man addressed her. She wasn't used to being addressed that way. She knew the role of dispatcher was originally filled by a priestess, but over time many people had come to the profession. At the moment of dispatch, the dispatcher was always addressed as Lady, no matter if male, female, or actual Priestess.

Brenna opened her heart as she gazed back at him. There was no fear in his face. As he thanked her, she gave him the injection in the chest. He drew a long deep breath, his first in days, then lay back on the bed, smiling. "Thank you, Brenna, the pain is gone."

He drew another long deep breath then passed as it left his body. He was still smiling. Nine beds and nine more farewells later, Brenna returned to her hut and sobbed her eyes out on Edie's shoulder.

Brenna was quite subdued the next day. Most everyone at the camp kept their distance. Few men were eager to look into the eyes that might be the last ones they ever see. She heard them whisper her name and in the same breath call her the "Angel of Death." For a woman who loved life, this was hard to hear.

Edie was her constant companion and the sisterly bond between them grew stronger. They were determined to help each other and survive together until Lessa and Micha returned to take them away.

The battle for Kora Six intensified and the wounded kept coming in an unending stream. Brenna emptied her kit repeatedly and each time the commander brought her fresh supplies. She was stunned to see how many re-fills the commander had in stores. Had he brought as many medicines, he might not have had such a great need for a dispatcher.

Kuris Morn

There was no indication on Lessa's face that she was disturbed by the smell of sweat emanating from her new company. Neither she nor the men seemed to notice the growing stench. All were focused on whether their plan would work. If they thought they'd been crowded aboard the freighter, they now realized what cramped meant as they hurtled through the atmosphere in the tiny fighter. It was a hot rough ride, but their ruse worked. They made it to the planet undetected.

The fighter swooped gracefully to a soft landing and the hatch flew open. Six hardened warriors, armed to the teeth, spilled out and quickly secured the area. Micha led Lessa out of the ship.

"All right, we're on Kuris Morn," Zartah said as he continued to search the horizon for any sign their landing had been detected. "Where do we go from here?"

"I'll seek the exact location in a moment," Lessa replied as she stretched the kinks out of her back.

"It was pretty cozy in there." Micha grinned as he too stretched himself. Lessa sank to a cross legged position on the ground and placed her hands flat on the soil. She began breathing deeply and her eyes went out of focus.

Micha stood guard beside her, and the troops all faced outwards away from her. They had spent many days close to the high priestess and were now her loyal soldiers and mercenaries no longer. Finally Lessa opened her eyes and rose to her feet.

"We're a long way from where we need to be. There's a range of mountains to the west of here. Somewhere along that range is a peak that's snow bound all year round. It is the only one like it on this planet. We must go there.

"Hmm, Bein Breah," mused Micha. "We could see it in the distance from our farm. It's to the south west, I think."

"You know the area, Micha?"

"Somewhat. I was rarely allowed to leave the farm, but ... We're on the eastern edge of the farming plains. It'll take many days to walk across to the mountain wall."

"How many?"

"About a season's worth, I'd guess."

Lessa chuckled at that. "Gorda, do you have any recommendations?"

"We can fly below sensor range at night. It'll be dangerous with so many aboard, but the chances of marching unseen across open land for a season are slim at best."

"Agreed. I'll do what I can to hide our passage."

"We'll use thrusters only, relatively no noise to alert sharp ears."

They settled down to wait for darkness. Lessa noticed the faraway look on Micha's face. "Your thoughts are far from here, friend Micha. They rest upon a certain girl with straight black hair and warm lips, perhaps?"

He chuckled and turned to her. "It was her eyes, Lessa. We needed a diversion, so I jumped in and claimed her just to start a fuss. It worked well, but she has courage and wouldn't run away when I gave her the chance. She stayed and protected my back.

"I admired that, but it was what I saw in her eyes. When she looked back at me, I suddenly wanted to make the claim real. I know we've never met before, but it's like we recognized something special in each other in a little more than a heartbeat. I was surprised when she actually agreed to be claimed.

"Lessa, when you think of Miss O'Loran, what is it that comes to mind first?"

"The scent of her hair, Micha," smiled Lessa. "I can close my eyes, think of her, and I swear I can detect the scent of her hair."

"Should we have stayed?"

"We couldn't, nor can I return yet. Micha, you may return if you wish. You didn't know..."

"I'm not leaving you alone, Lessa. In all my short life, you were the first besides my parents to show me kindness. I was born a slave, yet you, the highest of the high, have always treated me as an equal. For that, you will always have my loyalty. What I don't understand is, why me."

"The bounty hunter was cruel and all others were afraid, but you risked your life to share food and water with me. You had no idea who I was, yet you took the chance anyway. It was a noble act and spoke of great courage. It was an act that marks you as more than worthy to be my friend. We're not high priestess and guardian; we're Micha and Lessa, friends and equals. We'll always be thus."

"Thank you, Lessa." Micha smiled and added, "If you don't mind, I'll go back to thinking about Edie's eyes now."

As darkness fell they climbed aboard the fighter and headed out across the plains. They were in luck as it was a moonlit night. Gorda was able to fly darkened so there were no tell-tale lights in the sky. As dawn broke, they reached the mountain range. By midmorning they reached the tallest peak.

"We're here, Lessa. Where do we head next?"

"About halfway up there'll be a cavern, Micha. We must climb and find it. I have hopes it will be large enough for the fighter to land in. That'll keep the ship well hidden, and it'll be easier to defend if we're discovered."

They headed up the trail and, sometime later, they found the cavern. The entrance was well hidden, but big enough to accommodate the ship. They didn't want any electronic communication to alert the Arlens to their presence, so Micha returned to give directions. Lessa was waiting in the large cavern as Gorda easily brought the ship inside and landed.

Again the hatch flew open and armed warriors swarmed out to secure the area. "Where do we go now, Lessa?" Micha was grinning. He liked exploring caves.

"Back there, Micha, but I must go alone. That which I seek is hidden and protected with spells. Only I can approach. I don't know what will happen here or how long I'll be gone. I could return in mere moments, it may take days, and it may take much longer. If I don't return by the time your supplies run low, leave this planet and find safety."

"We won't leave you behind, Lessa."

"You will do as I bid you, Micha. I want you to remain safe, not perish of starvation or old age here on this mountain. Do as I ask you."

"Yes, Lady, your bidding shall be done." Lessa turned away for she knew he lied. Micha just shook his head and grinned. He would not leave, even it if took her years to return, and they both knew it. Lessa walked back into the depths of the cavern and vanished into the darkness. Eight days later the supplies ran out.

⸻⸻●⸻⸻

AS LESSA FELT HERSELF enclosed by total darkness, she spoke the first spell. A light appeared to show the way. She was no longer within the cavern. Following the light along a dim corridor, she continually repeated the next spell in her mind. There would be no second chance should she misspeak.

The corridor ended at a blank wall. She spoke the spell to reveal that which was hidden. The air crackled and sparked as a doorway slowly appeared in the wall. Lessa pushed against the huge slabs of stone and they moved aside for her. She took three steps forward beyond the threshold.

Lessa was back inside the dusty old library! She spun around taking in as much as she could all at once. The place was much like she remembered it. Now, where to begin? Hours passed and Lessa eventually fell asleep reading. When she awakened, her hunger and thirst made her wish she'd brought some refreshment with her.

She returned to the entrance and opened the door. This time she saw no corridor, only a stone wall. She was trapped inside! Panic rose in her breast, but she fought against it. There had to be a way. The old witch was reputed to be in here for months without supplies. Breathing deeply and focusing her mind, Lessa spoke firmly.

"Bring to me food and water." There was a creaking, grinding sound as something moved that had not moved for generations. Finally a dais rose from the floor, a full water jug and fresh fruit lay upon it.

A voice sounded from the ether, "That was the first lesson. State your needs clearly and they will be met."

"Who are you? Where are you?" There came no answer. "Perhaps I've triggered a spell. Very well, state my needs clearly," she thought as she chewed slowly on a piece of apple. "All right, it could take me years to learn even half of what is here, and even then it might not be of help."

"I need guidance." "What do you seek?" asked the voice. "My needs are many and complex. I seek the maker of this library."

"Beware what you ask, for you well might receive it. Are you strong enough to withstand her power?"

"I know not, but there is no other way. I also know this is no spell, but the witch of the library herself to whom I speak."

There was a loud cackling laugh at this. "Well done, girl, when are you?"

"What do you mean, when am I?"

"Only a true descendant of mine could access this portion of the temple library. How many generations have passed since my death?"

"Nine."

"Nine? I'd truly love to look upon the temple as it is in your time." Slowly the air thickened and a woman about twice Lessa's age appeared. "Shall we look through the window together?"

"We're not in the temple."

"Where then?"

"I don't know. The regent and the council moved the library shortly after I found it as a child. I was forbidden to enter again, and then it was gone."

"Hid my private library? Why?"

"They say no one should ever be allowed to wield the dark power again."

"The dark power? What do you mean, the dark power?" she was getting agitated and Lessa became wary.

"Lady, please tell me of your position in the temple."

"Norlene, my name is Norlene. I'm the high priestess, and this is my library. It's located in the temple on Borealis Prime."

"Lady, how did you avoid the marriage to the Viceroy?"

"The Viceroy? Why in the nine hells of Porapix would I want to marry a politician?"

"You were not forced?"

"Forced? Are you serious?" She fumed for a moment then drew a deep breath and calmed herself. "It seems much has changed since my time. I was afraid of that. It always happens when you time shift too much, and I confess I did a lot of that at first. I imagine you have much to tell me."

"I'm Arlessa, high priestess of the temple. In my time a girl is promoted to high priestess then she reigns for three years before joining the Viceroy's harem. At the day of her marriage, an inhibitor is implanted in her brain to control her and negate all her power."

"What? You allow this?" Norlene was now trembling with rage.

"I do not. I've put a temporary stop to it."

"Explain yourself. What do you mean?"

"I fled the temple. They can't appoint another high priestess until I've been missing for three years. I reappear every year or so then vanish again. I'm hunted by the Viceroy and his minions as well as by the ruling council of the temple."

The woman was quiet now, listening carefully. Lessa could see the vast intellect behind those eyes was hard at work. "Where do you go?"

"I join the mercenaries and go to the battle fronts to work as healer and dispatcher."

"Wars? The companies allow wars?"

"The companies started the wars about twenty years past with the destruction of Nova Prime."

The woman fell back and leaned against the wall. "Nova Prime destroyed? How? Why?" Norlene collected herself, wiping her hand across her face and then smoothing her robes. "Forgive my manners, Arlessa. Please tell me all."

Norlene leaned heavily against the arm of a chair as she lowered herself into it. She gestured for Lessa to sit in the chair closest to her. Cautiously, Lessa sat then picked up the threads of her tale.

"It was after your disappearance. A new priestess came to power, but she was weak and easily controlled by the companies. Before her reign was ended Nova Prime was made a slave world as punishment for you becoming the Black Witch."

"Black Witch? Me?"

"The winners write the histories. You were the last high priestess to wield true power. They say it consumed you and that is why you vanished."

"So, I became the reason to remove that power, at least politically," Norlene sighed and rubbed her temples. "Tell me of Nova Prime."

"Nova remained a slave world until shortly after the time of my birth. She declared independence, but the companies threw up a blockade then dumped poisonous gasses into the atmosphere. Every living breathing thing on the planet died, including my parents. I was kept safe by the Nara Clan of Borealis."

Norlene didn't speak for several moments. Lessa watched the muscles working along her jaw as the Black Witch fought to control the emotions rising within her. At last she nodded her head slowly and then sighed again. "Nara Clan, I always did like that bunch of free thinkers. What happened after the massacre?"

"The entire sector rose up against the companies and drove them out. Now the region is run by different groups - warlords, kings, etc. who all fight among themselves. Alliances change overnight, but the wars go on. I seek the last of the Novans. They're scattered about the sector, working as mercenaries mostly."

"That's why you prowl the battle fronts. You're trying to reunite the people."

"Yes, but it's difficult as I must avoid the marriage to the Viceroy."

"There is also another reason, is there not? What's her name?"

"How did you know it is a woman?"

"That has ever been the main thought of a Novan witch," Norlene replied, smiling.

"Her name is Brenna O'Loran."

Lessa could feel herself warming to this powerful woman. "You've been apart a long time, yet you come seeking me, why?"

"I was only in this library for a short time as a child, yet I learned enough to make me the strongest of the priestesses in training."

"So they promoted you to get rid of you. You're here to learn more. You seek more power."

"Yes, enough to survive and fulfill my purpose."

"Which is?"

"Restore Nova."

Norlene sighed and thought for a moment. "The entire atmosphere is poisoned?"

"Yes."

"All right, Arlessa. To do this will take both of us at full strength. I need a bit of practice and you need significant instruction. Here's what I propose, I'll train you and we'll then work together on this. Is this acceptable to you?"

"It is. I couldn't have hoped for so much. Thank you, Norlene."

"Don't thank me yet, girl. You may well not survive the training. To gain true power you must release the darkness within you and embrace it while you integrate it into the whole being that you are. If you do survive you'll be changed forever. Are you willing to face that? Will she be?" Norlene took Lessa's hands into hers and searched the young witch's face for signs of hesitation.

Lessa's heart swelled as she spoke. "I believe in her, she will accept. I must do this, Norlene."

"Then we begin..."

⸻⸻◈⸻⸻

BACK ON THE MOUNTAIN top, Lessa's company faced its own challenges. When the supplies ran out, Gorda took the troops and left, vowing to find a second ship and return. Zartah and Micha remained behind.

"So, little brother, what do we do for food now? That left leg of yours looks tasty."

"Perhaps it does, but you're much bigger than I am. I could stay alive much longer by eating you than you could by eating me."

Zartah roared with laughter at that. "Sound logic, Micha, have you any other suggestions? I'd prefer not to be roasted on a spit."

"I'm familiar with this planet. You stay here in case Lessa returns. I'll go see what food I can find." With that he swept up his weapons and left the cavern.

Micha returned the next morning with a large backpack filled with food. "There's an abandoned farm about three hours march from the mountain. They must have left recently, and quickly, based on how much they left behind, and little has spoiled as yet. There could be soldiers nearby, but I didn't see any."

He tossed his companion a piece of fruit. "You're a most resourceful young fellow, Micha. Consider me your man, that is, if you're willing to accept me."

"Zartah?"

"I was reflecting while you were gone. Everyone knows it's a better life to follow a good leader than to fail alone. As a leader I failed and lost my crew. As a freeman, I was forever getting into trouble, as the location of our first meeting will testify. Since we met, Micha, I have had my freedom and exciting things to do. I'm well fed and content. I would be your first man if you'll have me."

Micha sighed and leaned his back against the cavern wall. "Zartah, I've barely seen seventeen summers, yet, with Lessa's time shifting, it has been nineteen years since the time of my birth out on that plain. At seventeen, a man can carry weapons, which I do, and at nineteen he can lead men. If this is truly your wish, I accept. Be aware that service to the high priestess can be a dangerous path to walk."

"As I said, always something exciting to do."

"Fine, then since I haven't slept since I left, you get the first watch."

Zartah just grinned and turned his attention to the mouth of the cavern. Micha sank lower and drifted off to sleep. The days passed slowly for the two men. They watched, practiced hand to hand combat techniques, and talked. Eventually Micha had to make another trip to the abandoned farm. He left early the following morning leaving Zartah with orders to stay at base camp until Lessa or Gorda and the others returned.

Three hours later, Micha reached the farm again, but this time a squad of soldiers was waiting for him. Micha saw them first and hid from view for several hours. Eventually he tried to slip around them but was spotted. In the firefight that followed three soldiers were killed before Micha was finally captured and got the butt end of a rifle in the back of his head.

Back at base camp, Gorda and one other, the silent woman warrior, had returned. Zartah explained the cache that Micha had found at the abandoned farm. It was agreed that Zartah and the woman should head out there to see what they could scavenge. If soldiers were in the vicinity, it may not be wise to make another trip back there.

Keira, the woman warrior, agreed to go with him. While she couldn't provide the banter with which Zartah had become accustomed, she kept pace with him and proved to be an able tracker. They had stopped to eat when the echo of weapons fire rolled across the plain.

"Did you hear that Keira?" His companion nodded as she quickly stowed her rations in her pack. "It seems Micha was right to be worried about soldiers."

They moved carefully then, Zartah hoped they wouldn't be too late. Darkness forced them to wait until morning. They set out again, careful to avoid being seen.

That morning, a manacled Micha was pulled to his feet. His captors pushed a shovel at him and had him dig a hole big enough to bury their comrades. As he replaced the last shovel full of earth, he felt the rifle butt make contact between his shoulders and he hit the ground heavily.

They brutally interrogated him for the next hour. Clearly they thought he was some sort of scout or spy. When it was plain they would get nothing useful from him, they staked him out naked on the ground in full sun. "When the shadow from that building crosses you, you will die. You have until then to talk."

The day was hot and Micha's battered body was burned by the time the shadow reached him. As the soldiers approached him, he closed his eyes and thought of Edie. The remaining soldiers squared off and raised their weapons, but had no time to fire.

Zartah and the woman warrior charged around the building, screaming a battle challenge, and gunning them down. Micha's would-be executioners had no chance.

"Come on, boss, let's get you in the shade and get some clothes on you."

"Water!" Micha croaked.

"Coming right up." Zartah trotted away then soon returned with a canister of water. "Drink up now."

"Zartah, how...?"

"Sound carries well out here in the open. We thought we heard the gunfire and came running. It took a while to find you but looks like we arrived in time. See, always something exciting to do on your crew."

"Yes you did. You're a good man, Zartah, and you'll be rewarded."

"Oh?"

"Yes. I'm too burned to carry the food, so you get to carry it. Since you're so much bigger and stronger than I am, we can take back much more food. Extra rations for you."

"You're just too good to me, Micha," grinned Zartah as he helped the boy to stand. "Let's get going and head back."

They gathered as much as Zartah could carry and set out for the cavern. Micha led the way, Zartah close behind, and Keira guarding the rear. The going was slow as Micha couldn't move fast and had to stop for water often.

When they finally reached the cavern a day later they found Gorda standing guard and two new long-range Arcalian fighter ships fully armed. Micha sank to the ground, gingerly put his back to the wall, and rested his head. Even with Lessa's enhancements, the climb had nearly finished him. He only half listened as Zartah related his adventure to Gorda.

It took him a moment to realize the woman was squatting quietly near him, waiting for him to acknowledge her. When he made eye contact, she pointed to Zartah then to Micha. Then she patted her own chest then pointed to Micha.

"Keira wants to join your crew, Micha." Zartah said softly. "She can't talk. The Arlens cut out her tongue a couple of years ago." Micha looked her in the eyes again. "The pay is terrible." She chuckled and repeated her motions. "All right, Keira, if you're sure, I'm thrilled to have a fighter of your skill watching my back." She smiled and patted his shoulder, then turned and took the watch at the entrance.

Gorda approached and grinned. "Got room for me on that crew?"

"Why, Gorda? You're a crew boss yourself. Why serve a kid who can't pay?"

"Well, first you stole my last pilot, and second you saved my life. I'm Nara clan, and you brought me out of that prison where I was about to die of torture. You kept us all together, led us out, took us north, and found folk who could see everybody safe. My luck has improved immensely since we met. In truth, I guess I've been your man since then.

"Micha, I've had little purpose in life so far except to get in trouble. You're a man with a higher purpose. At this stage of my life, I want that too. I bring two fighter ships fully armed and ready. How about it?"

Micha just shook his head. "Imagine, three grown warriors throwing their lot in with me," he thought. "Welcome aboard then everyone. Zartah is first man, you're the specialist, and Keira is our super trooper." She chuckled from the entrance and gave him a bright smile, a wink, then turned back to watch. It took several days for his sunburn to ease and bruised muscles to fully heal. Then the peeling of damaged skin began.

Micha looked like a snake with a half shed skin. He chafed and rubbed against the sides of the cavern, the rough edges of the fighters, and used anything he could find to shove down the back of his shirt to ease the itching. When the food ran out again, Zartah and Gorda prepared to go for more.

"Take a ship, Zartah."

"Micha?"

"Take a ship. You can carry more back with you, and you can be there and back in less time than you can reach the bottom of the mountain on foot. The ship's sensors can also tell you if there are enemies about. We don't need any more trouble."

"Right boss. A ship it is. You pilot, Gorda. I'll watch for company." Gorda snorted and climbed into the pilot's seat. A moment later the ship rose gracefully and swept out into the night. When they returned they were grinning from ear to ear.

"What are you two so excited about?"

"Payday Micha! It's payday!" Zartah grinned.

"What are you talking about?"

"Well, we were gathering food and other supplies when we found the transport your former friends had used. It looks like they were deserters who were looting the abandoned farms. There's a lot of interplanetary script here, more than enough to refuel the ships, recharge the weapons, and still give the crew a year's pay."

"You're joking."

"I'm not. So, what do you want to do?"

"Split it into five shares, Zartah, a share for each and a share for future expenses. Does that sound reasonable to everybody?"

"I'd say that's a bit overly generous, Boss," said Gorda. "No crew gets paid a full share."

"Mine does. You were all ready to share in nothing, now you share equally in this. First man, split it up and share it out."

"Aye, boss. See, Gorda, always excitement and we get paid well. What more could you want?"

<hr>

TWO DAYS LATER LESSA strode out of the back of the cavern. She was hard eyed and dressed in black robes. "Lessa," shouted Micha as he started towards her, but his voice died in the air as he saw her eyes. "Are you all right, Lessa?"

"I may be, in time. It's been years, Micha, how are you?"

"Years, Lessa? It's been but a season here."

"Time behaves differently where I've been. Are you well?"

"I am. Lessa..."

He got no further as she suddenly seized him in a bear hug, tears streaming down her face. Micha held her gently until the storm of emotion passed. "Micha, there were so many times I was afraid I wouldn't be able to return. It's so good to see your smiling face once again, dear friend. You waited a full season for me?"

"I promised to wait, Lessa. I set no limits on that. I'm your guardian, and it was my task to wait for your return. It's so good to see you again. I've missed you terribly."

They just gazed at each other for a while then Micha spoke again. "I gather that you found it?"

"Oh yes, and much more. I'm now far better prepared for the task at hand."

"Would you like to rest a few days before we go? You look tired, Lessa."

"I am tired, Micha. Perhaps you're right, I do need to rest. We'll wait one more day, and then we go home to Kora Six."

"We wait one more day, Zartah. On the morrow, prepare everything for leaving."

"Aye boss."

"Boss? You're crew boss now?"

"Ah...yes."

"Sit here, Micha. You have a tale to tell, and I do want to hear it." She rested her back against the wall as he softly spoke. Lessa listened to the voice of her young friend and allowed tears to leak from her eyes. It had been so long, and she had been to so many dark places, but she'd survived.

Norlene was a hard teacher, but she had willingly shared what she knew, holding nothing back. Even as Lessa sat with Micha, she knew Norlene was on Nova Prime, clearing the atmosphere.

Dispatcher

Brenna gazed absent-mindedly at the dispatcher's kit resting on the floor beside her small bunk. Was that the fifth refill, or the sixth? She could no longer remember. The fatigue was deep in her body and her soul. How many lives had she ended? How many soldiers dead by her hand? Brenna had lost count.

Even as Brenna's soul shrank from the task she had to perform, her reputation among the soldiers grew. None had ever seen a dispatcher so compassionate. Brenna took time to speak with each man, look into his eyes and hold him gently as she took his life.

Edie lay sleeping and Brenna reached over to pull the thin blanket back over her. Edie now wore the red and white uniform of a full medic. She had passed the field exam a week prior, and now they were rarely on the same shift. The men were now more respectful of Edie too. There was no point annoying a medic who roomed with the dispatcher.

A soft tapping came at the door. "It's time, ladies."

"Time?" asked Edie, as she pushed herself upright and yawned. "How long did I sleep?"

"Not long enough, honey," sighed Brenna, "but here we go. We're working the same shift for a change."

"Maybe it'll be a quiet night."

"That would be refreshing."

"Brenna, why don't you take the medic's exam? You could pass it easily. Leave this to another, you've done more than enough."

Brenna just smiled sadly and shook her head. "No, I won't ask another to do this. Let's go." They ducked out the door and headed for the big infirmary. There were wounded everywhere, outside on cots, some on stretchers and a few just lying on the ground, waiting to be seen.

"Looks like I'll have another busy night," Edie sighed.

"Yes, me too, sadly. Find me for a meal later?"

"I should be clear by ten. Brenna..."

"I have thought about it, Edie; it would be easier on me, but not for them. Some have told me horror stories of things they have seen on the battlefields. If they must be released from life early, it is better they see a friendly face when they go."

"I suppose you're right. I could take the oath and do every other night to give you a break."

"Thank you, Edie, but It's bad enough that one of us must do this. You're too young to wear this burden."

"I'm stronger than you think, Brenna."

"I know, but I want to unite you with Micha without the weight of all this bearing down on you."

"Sometimes I worry he won't come. There's so much war and death. How can he ever get through it all to find me?"

"You know well who he's with. She'll bring him through, she will bring him through." Brenna looked up and saw the commander coming toward them, his face a hard mask.

"Eight more tonight, Brenna."

"I'll need a refill for my kit in the morning."

"I just got a new supply; you'll have your refill."

Brenna watched him walk away, a hard look in her eye. "Damn that man, he's got me killing more of his men than the Arlens. Wherever you are, Lessa my love, please return for me." Her shoulders sagged as she walked toward the long building that had once been a barn and was now the hospice. It would be a long night once again.

As dawn came she met Edie outside the food tent. The air was strangely quiet. Suddenly a bomb exploded nearby shattering the calm. The witch's spell had failed at last. The camp was instantly in chaos; the commander was bawling orders and people raced about everywhere. Bombers roared overhead, and tracer fire streaked across the sky from just outside the farm complex.

Transports were being loaded with wounded and pulling out. Brenna and Edie sought the shelter of their hut, but they knew it wouldn't stand up if the bombs struck any closer. The commander stuck his head through the door. "Hurry, we don't have much time."

"Time for what, Commander?"

"To get out, for the love of the gods, woman, come on!"

"I'm not going anywhere."

"Brenna, don't be a fool. The Arlen troops will be here in minutes. They won't be as easy going as I've been. You can't stay here. Your mates can find you with your kin on the new farm."

"Go," said Edie, "we will remain."

"Two bloody fools," he muttered as he leaped into his transport and roared away. Soon the farm was deserted and eerily silent.

"I wonder, should we have gone with them?"

"It's too late for a second guess, Edie. We've got company coming."

A solid wave of heavily armed ground vehicles and fully loaded troop carriers came roaring over the hill in a cloud of dust. They rolled up to the two women standing at the edge of the farm. The troops swarmed over the farm and through the buildings; three aimed their weapons at the Edie and Brenna.

The girls didn't move, neither did they speak. At length a small transport arrived and a man in a gaudy uniform with a chest full of medals stepped to the ground.

"Report!" he barked as a man ran up to and saluted him.

"The area is secured, sir. All buildings abandoned except the long barn which was used as a hospice. There are several badly wounded men still there. They didn't have time to move or dispatch them."

"What about those two women?"

"Unknown, sir. They were right there as we arrived. I put them under guard, nothing more."

"Bring them to me."

The man signaled and the guards pushed the two women forward until they stood before the one giving the orders. "Who are you?"

"I'm Brenna O'Loran, and this is Edie."

"Why did the Maccay leave you behind? To spy on us perhaps?"

"We aren't spies. We were left behind because we refused to go."

"Really? Why did you do that?"

"Our mates were off world when the battles began. We must be here when they return, how else would they find us?"

"A most likely story." He snorted then turned to the guard. "Throw them in the slave pens with the others. Kill those in the barn. We'll use this hospice for our own wounded."

Brenna jerked her arm free of the man who had grabbed her. "Wait. I'm a dispatcher, and my friend is a medic. We would be of more use to you here than sold as slaves."

"So you are spies," the officer retorted.

"We aren't spies. We wish only to remain until our mates return for us. We don't owe allegiance to either side in this conflict, nor do we claim these lands for our own. We wish only to remain until we're reunited with our mates. We'll willingly do the same work for you as we did for the Maccay. We only want to stay here."

The officer regarded Brenna carefully. She didn't flinch. "Damned if I'm not starting to believe you. All right, if you're a dispatcher, where's your kit?"

"In our hut, over there. There are only three charges left. It needs a refill."

He snapped his fingers and a soldier raced to the hut and soon returned with her kit as well as Edie's med kit. "I'm Commandant Kazak," he said as he looked over the two kits. "All right ladies, you're hired. We'll supply your needs, food and clothing as well, and you may remain. Any sign of treachery, or if you try to escape, you will be shot. Are we agreed?"

"Agreed, Commandant Kazak."

"You may keep the same hut. Now, get busy and clear out that hospice for me, I have wounded too you know." He was walking away as he spoke. Brenna and Edie gathered their kits and headed for the barn.

A soldier was waiting at the door with a fresh Arlen dispatch kit for Brenna. She took it and entered the building. There were nearly a dozen beds with wounded men still in them. Each also had a soldier with a weapon aimed at the man in the bed.

Brenna drew a deep breath and, taking out the first charge, stepped forward. "I'll deal with this. You men step back away from the beds."

The big soldier nearest to her spun with alarming speed and grabbed her by the throat. "You give no orders here, you Maccay slut. I should break your neck for daring to speak to an Arlen soldier." Brenna was choking and trying to pry away his fingers.

Edie had started forward, but several weapons were instantly aimed at her. "As a matter of fact, I think I will." He snarled in her face as he tightened his grip, then suddenly looked down at the syringe she had driven into his side. A heartbeat later he sank to the floor, dead.

Brenna was trembling, as she gasped for air. At length she regained her breath then glared at the rest of the soldiers. "The next man who touches me or my friend will meet the same fate, now do as I say and step back." One of the men looked her in the eye for a moment then he shouldered his weapon. "Stepping back, Ma'am. Permission to remove the body of Morad."

"Granted."

The man signaled and two others picked up the body of the soldier and removed it. Brenna started toward the first bed, still trembling. Edie caught her arm and passed her a tablet. "This will calm your nerves and let you function."

"Thank you, Edie," she murmured as she swallowed the medication. Brenna drew a few deep breaths then sat beside the first man. It had begun. She took her time with each man, giving him time to make his peace and say goodbye. It was late when they finished and stepped from the building. An armed squad of men was waiting.

They were taken to a tent with a flag flying atop, the Commandant's tent. As soon as they were inside, the commandant turned to a soldier standing at his desk. It was one of the men from the barn. "Speak."

"That woman killed squad leader Morad. The entire squad was witness."

"Is this true?" He had turned and spoken to Brenna.

"Yes."

"I told you to dispatch the wounded in the beds, not my troops. What happened?"

"I told the armed men to step away from the beds so I could work. He grabbed me by the throat and choked me. He said he was going to break my neck. I stuck him with a syringe."

"Soldier, is this accurate?"

"Yes, sir."

"What's done is done then. Morad's taste for the aggression drugs was beginning to make him a liability."

"Sir, the penalty for killing a soldier is death..."

"The penalty, Soldier, is whatever I deem it to be, understood?"

"Sir?"

"Soldier, how long has it been since we had a medic or dispatcher with us?"

"Weeks, sir. Months possibly."

"How many of our people have died screaming because there was no medic to help them or dispatcher to ease their passing?"

"Far too many, sir. We requisition them, but they just keep sending medical and dispatching supplies that no one has the skills to use."

"Exactly. The women's penalty will be to work for us. They're to be treated respectfully. They're not to be harmed and they're not to leave the compound."

"Aye, sir." The man saluted and left the tent, signaling the others to leave as well. Brenna and Edie were left alone with the Commandant. "Drink, ladies?" he asked as he took out a bottle and poured one for himself. "Brenna, is it?"

"Water please."

"Won't drink with an Arlen?"

"It's not that. The drink will weaken my resolve. I dare not if I'm to function."

"Understood. You, Edie was it?"

"Yes, my name is Edie. Water please."

"Fair enough." He passed them each a water container. He then tossed the fiery liquid down and poured himself another. "I took no pleasure in ordering what I did."

"Nor I in the doing."

"Agreed," he nodded. "What brought a high-born lady out to Kora Six, if I may ask?"

"The wars," sighed Brenna. "Wars have a way of putting people in places where they didn't expect to be. We were bound elsewhere when the ship was damaged. We sought refuge here and the farmers took us in. That was some time ago."

"Wars do indeed put folk in places, and positions, they didn't expect. All right, ladies. You both look exhausted; get some rest. Our wounded will start arriving in a few hours. We'll need you then." They thanked him for the water then returned to the hut. Edie held Brenna gently as she cried herself to sleep.

Edie had lived barely eighteen summers, yet she had seen more hard life than a young girl should, and she was waiting for the return of a seventeen year old warrior who had claimed her in the midst of armed slavers. Sadly, she was beginning to despair of his return.

———●———

MURTAH STRETCHED AND smiled as he watched the sun rise over the hills of his new farm. Ena came to stand beside him, and he put his arm around her waist. They watched the sunrise together. It was a good farm, this land they'd been given. Machinery and stock had been provided as well, and the Maccay had assisted in putting up new buildings. The first harvest was about ready, and Murtah was well pleased. Life was good.

They turned back to join the others at the morning meal. Everyone was chatting happily when suddenly a man who had gone outside returned on the run, cursing wildly. "Amon, what's going on?" "War's here. Two Arcalian long range fighters inbound." Every man grabbed a weapon of some kind.

Murtah stepped through the door to see the big birds swoop gracefully to a landing right before him. He braced himself for the worst as the hatch dropped open and a heavily armed man landed easily on the ground. He straightened up and looked hard at Murtah.

"A weapon? That's a damn poor greeting for a brother you haven't seen in years."

"Zartah? Is that really you?"

"It was last time I looked this morning."

"Zartah!" The two men were suddenly in each other's arms, pounding each other on the back, tears running freely down their faces. Another armed warrior dropped out of the fighter, stretched then stepped forward.

The second ship opened and a heavily armed, battle scarred woman dropped to the ground, weapons at the ready. She spun easily aside, a move that would have confounded an enemy trying to shoot her. Seeing no threat, she straightened up and smiled. Her smile changed her face from that of a hard bitten warrior to a beautiful woman. She reached up and rapped the side of the ship with her knuckles.

Another warrior dropped to the ground. "Micha!" Ena pounced on him and grabbed him in a bear hug. He hugged her back, grinning broadly. As Ena released him, Murtah gave him another bear hug.

"Better stay in the ship, Lessa," he called. "We've landed among a troupe of wrestlers. They're killing me."

"I'll take my chances," she laughed as she dropped easily to the ground.

"Lady," it was a group murmur as everyone knelt before her.

"Rise my friends, rise. This is no temple. Stand and greet me as a friend." She was looking all around, searching, as they greeted her.

"They're not here, Lady."

"What do you mean, Ena? Who isn't here?"

"Brenna and Edie, Lady. They're not here."

"What do you know of Edie?" asked Micha.

"We know much of your mate, Micha. Come inside everyone, we'll sit at table and give you all the news." When all were settled, Ena began her tale.

"It was a few weeks after you left. A girl wandered in to the farm, looking for Micha. She said he had chosen her and told the tale of how it came to be. We accepted her as your mate, Micha, and she lived with us for a full season or more. She's smart and a hard worker, Micha, you chose well."

"So, where did she go?"

"Nowhere. When the wars came to Kora Six, we were brought here by the Maccay and given this wonderful farm."

"So we heard," said Lessa. "That's why we've come. Tell us why Brenna and Edie aren't here with you."

"Lady, they wouldn't come." Ena was looking at her hands now, not meeting Lessa's eyes.

"What? Why not?"

"They were afraid you wouldn't be able to find them, so they stayed where they expected you to look for them. The Maccay took over the old farm and made a hospice out of it. We heard that Brenna was working as the dispatcher there, and Edie had become a medic."

"Oh Brenna, your poor soft heart..."

"There's more, Lady. The Arlens overran the farm, but Brenna and Edie wouldn't leave with the Maccay during the evacuation. As far as we know they're in the hands of the Arlens now, if they survived."

Micha's fist hit the table with a crash. "Keira, Gorda, take what script you need and get those ships re-fueled, rationed, and top up the weapons. We're going in."

"Aye, boss!" Gorda grinned as he rose to his feet. Keira patted Micha's shoulder, gave him a closed fist salute, and then jogged out the door. Murtah and the others looked surprised as Micha took command.

"Boss, shall I see if I can find a few volunteers?"

"Zartah, I release you from the bond."

"Release me? I'm fired? Less than a season as first man and I'm fired?"

"I thought you might prefer to remain with Murtah. After being apart for so many years, I thought..."

"I'm not letting you go into battle without me. Forget that. Lady, tell him."

"I think he gets it, Zartah. Micha is right, though. Are you certain about this?"

"Lady, my luck changed the day I met Micha and has been even better since I joined his crew. If the crew goes in; I go in."

"All right then," said Micha. "We all go in, but no volunteers, Zartah, not for this. I need hardened warriors, folk I know and trust. Lessa, can I talk you into staying here in safety?"

"No."

"Thought not."

"I'll go too if you'll have me on your crew, Micha."

"Murtah..."

"No, Micha," said Ena, gently patting his hand. "He's been tortured ever since you disappeared. When Edie said you were with the Lady, he relaxed a bit, but he's been tormented since we left those girls behind. He's a good fighter, my Murtah."

"Murtah, you were like a father to me, you taught me what I know of combat. You know there can only be one crew boss. Can you follow me?"

"I can, Micha. I can see these warriors follow you without question and there has to be good reasons for that devotion. You're the boss, I have no issues here."

"Welcome to the crew. Now, your task will be to stay here and protect these folk until we return." Murtah's eyes hardened and he straightened up. Lessa put her hand on Micha's arm. "You wouldn't stay, Micha, remember."

"All right, I know when I'm beaten. Have you weapons, Murtah? If not we'll supply you."

"I have weapons."

"Prepare then. You'll ride with Zartah and Gorda. Zartah's first man, Gorda is our specialist."

"The woman, Keira, looks like a stone cold killer until she smiles. Does she never speak?"

"She can't, the Arlens cut out her tongue. Apparently, she enjoyed singing too much."

"Are you going to make her go in there, even though the Arlens have control of it?" asked Ena.

"I couldn't stop her, Ena. She's appointed herself my bodyguard; besides, a chance for some payback is what she'll want. Our Keira truly is a warrior to be reckoned with."

"You've changed in the past two years, Micha."

"Two years? Lessa?"

"There was a time ripple as I entered the library, and a bigger one as we came out. It's probably been two years."

"I'm getting old too damn fast." Everyone was having a good chuckle as Micha shook his head sadly and Lessa ruffled his hair. While they waited for the ships to return, Lessa blessed the land. They felt the flow of her energy this time, for Lessa had grown much more powerful.

Lessa's tattoos glowed and energy flowed from her hands to the welcoming soil as the people looked on. The next day the ships returned, but within an hour blasted off again. They flew out of Maccay space in the company of several Maccan supply ships, entering the war zone at full burn.

Reunited

Zartah and Keira stood quietly by while Micha paced back and forth. They were in the commander's tent and Micha wasn't getting the answers he wanted.

"I am sorry young man, I just can't help you."

"You stole our home, our women did your dirty work for you for months, and now you won't raise a hand to help me retrieve them?"

"I can't risk hundreds of my men on a raid deep into Arlen territory, especially since we have no idea if they're alive or dead. They could be in the slave pens and sold by now."

"They're alive and they're still there where you left them," said Micha.

"How can you be so certain? What information do you have?"

"I have my sources. Help me, Commander. I brought your supply ships in through the blockade without a single loss. You owe me."

"The high command will pay your price, mercenary. Your people were relocated to a safe place, but those two refused to leave, not once, but twice. I won't risk my men on this. The discussion is closed."

Micha's hands opened and closed repeatedly as though he was choking the life from the commander. "So be it but know this. If you hinder me in any way, I'll hunt you to the end of your days. There'll be no place safe for you to hide from me. Come crew, we'll leave these brave men to their little war. We have people to find."

"Boy, if you cross into Arlen territory our people will consider you spies and fire upon you." The commander was shocked at the speed with which Micha reached him. They were standing nose to nose.

"We're friends of the Maccay, Commander. You'd be wise to make no effort to change that. We will enter Arlen territory, we will find our people, and we will bring them out. Use your head and think, this could be the diversion you need to regain some ground."

He spun on his heel and marched out of the tent. As they entered the tent they'd been given, Gorda was first to see the set of Micha's jaw. "You all right, boss?"

"I'm fine!" Micha sighed as he shook off the rage that threatened to consume him. "It went about as you expected, Lessa. We're on our own. The idiot actually threatened to fire on us if we crossed into Arlen territory."

"It seems I must reveal myself after all."

"Not just yet. Gorda, this is your type of action. What do you suggest we do?"

"If it were me, I'd have the two ships buzz the place a few times then one land to drop off the crew. The ships would keep the Arlens entertained while the crew found the targets and brought them out overland. The ships could then pick up the passengers at a safe distance."

"Sounds like a plan, we'll do it. Gorda, you never did tell us where you got the two Arcalian fighters."

"Long ago, I saved the life of a very powerful man. I never called in the favor until now. It seemed like the right time to claim the debt. Boss, we should go in right at sunset. You know, the fighters coming out of the sun, guns blazing."

"Well then, we'd better get ready. It's nearly time."

<hr>

"BRENNA, WHAT IS IT?"

Sitting bolt upright in her bed, Brenna rubbed her eyes then tilted her head as though she were listening. She held up her hand for silence. A moment later she turned to Edie with a bright smile of excitement. She laid her finger against her lips in warning against making a sound.

"Get dressed and ready to travel, Edie," she whispered. "They're coming."

"What? Who's coming... Oh good gods, you mean?"

"Yes, Lessa spoke in my mind. She and Micha are coming for us, we must be ready."

A rap came at the door. "It's sundown, ladies. Time to rise and shine! You're on the night shift." "We're awake," replied Edie. "How's the food today?"

"You can eat it," the soldier called as he walked away.

"What should we do, Brenna?"

"We get ready to go, but we wait here."

Both women dressed hurriedly and then sat on the beds to wait. Only a few minutes passed when they heard the air raid warning claxon. A moment later they heard the scream of the two fighter ships racing overhead, strafing the ground as they passed. The fighter ships were quite agile for their size and they reversed for another run before a defense could be mounted.

"Arcalian fighters," shouted several voices at once. "They're attacking!"

"They're supposed to be neutral!" bellowed another voice.

The chaos was total as the fighters came back in, flying low out of the setting sun. They split apart right over the compound and streaked away, only to return, first one, then the other.

Brenna and Edie clung to each other as they opened the door and stepped outside. They wanted to make it easy for the raiders to find them. Suddenly Brenna grabbed Edie by the arm. "Back inside, Edie, they will come in the darkness."

The next hour passed slowly, the silence reigning as the compound waited for another attack. It came just when they were about to stand down from alert. The raider ships swept in low and strafed the ground as they passed overhead.

As they swept by on the second pass a soft knock came at the door, a familiar voice spoke, "Miss O'Loran?" Brenna threw open the door and flung herself into Micha's arms, tears streaming down her face. He hugged her for a moment then passed her to a heavily armed woman behind him.

Edie stood looking at him, not knowing what to do. It had been so long ago, and this hardened warrior was no boy.

Micha grinned at her. "Come to me, my girl." She threw herself into his arms. He hugged her tightly for a moment then spoke softly. "Come, Edie, we have to move fast." Leading her by the hand, Micha took her around the hut and out into the field. They quickly found the breach in the barbed wire perimeter.

An armed man was guarding it and Brenna was on the other side, silently sobbing into the shoulder of a tall golden haired woman. They fled across the field and into the hills as the two fighter ships kept the compound busy. As they crossed the first hill and the compound disappeared from sight, Micha signaled the fighters.

"Zartah, Gorda, accomplished and clear." The two ships banked and streaked away. They stopped to rest in the cover of the rocks. Brenna was still sobbing into the shoulder of the tall woman. This would be the high priestess the whole sector was hunting for; the mate Brenna had ached to see once again.

Edie was staring at Lessa who looked up and smiled. Edie knelt. "Edie, we're all friends here, and you're more than a sister to my beloved Brenna. Do not kneel. Come sit with us."

"Are you truly the high priestess?"

"I am."

"I never dreamed I would ever meet the high priestess."

"Well, you have now, and we'll be great friends, I promise."

"If Micha will keep me. He may not want to; we only met for a moment."

"Micha has thought of little else but you. He won't part with you now. He's risked his own life and the lives of his crew to get you back. Micha swore to return for you, Edie, and he's done so. I'm sorry it took so long to get here, but I was delayed on my journey."

"I hope I'm pleasing to him."

"You're more than pleasing to me," his voice sounded behind her. Edie spun around to see him smiling at her. "Come, walk with me. We have time to talk at last."

She accepted his hand and rose to walk beside him. He guided her carefully down the hill until they were out of hearing distance, the female warrior a respectful distance behind. Finally he stopped, turned and held her gently by the shoulders, gazing deeply into her eyes. "Micha, what is it?"

"When first we met, Lessa and I needed a diversion. I jumped in and uttered my claim to provide that."

"Are you saying you were not serious?"

"Not at first, I was just making a fuss to attract the slaver's attention."

"Are you releasing me?"

"Hush now. Let me speak before I lose my nerve. Edie, I wasn't serious until I saw your courage, strength, loyalty, and, before we parted, your beauty. I do not want to release you; I want to keep you. Having said that, I'll understand if you would prefer to..."

"No, Micha, no. You claimed me, you made the offer and I accepted. You'll never be rid of me in this lifetime." Suddenly she was in his arms, hugging him tightly as he hugged her in return.

"Edie, I..." She stopped his words with a kiss that lit his young body on fire. As they sank to the ground, tearing at each other's clothing, Keira grinned and turned away to keep watch. The young lovers would not be disturbed this night.

Brenna lay quiet in Lessa's arms at last, her emotions spent. "I'm not as strong as she is, Lessa. Edie held me together many times as we waited for you."

"Hush now, my darling, I know the price you paid to wait for me. I'm so sorry I couldn't come sooner. I would have time shifted, but that's caused so much trouble already, I dared not do it again just yet. Brenna, I know what you've had to do to survive. I'd take that from you if I could."

"No, it's all right. I had to do it, for those poor soldiers, for myself, and to know if I was truly strong enough to be your mate."

"Strong enough? My darling, I chose you not for your strength, but for your courage, your gentle compassion, your beauty..."

"Keep going..."

"Hush, oh shameless one," Lessa smiled and then looked straight ahead, her eyes darkening. "I've died a thousand deaths trying to get back to you."

"Lessa, why did you go?"

"Many reasons, all of which I will share with you as soon as we're back in a safe place. For now, just rest in my arms and let me hold you."

"Can I ask where you've been?"

"Far too many dark and evil places, places lost between realms and better left there. When we have the luxury of time I'll tell you what I can, but for now, just rest."

"None of it matters, Lessa. It only matters that you came for me." Once again the tears began as Brenna continued to release the burden of the past two years of her life. Eventually she drifted off to sleep, cuddled in her beloved's arms.

Further down the hill, Micha and Edie lay beside each other, deliciously sated. "Micha?"

"Yes, my love?" Edie smiled at the endearment.

"Was I all right for you?" she asked tentatively. Micha turned and stroked her face. "All right? You were perfect. You are perfect. My dearest Edie." His lips brushed hers then he pulled back. "Was I...?"

"You were all I dreamed you would be and more, my Micha." Edie rained sweet kisses on his face. "I will never let you leave me behind again. I want to be with you always." Micha wrapped his arms around Edie as he claimed her mouth again. He felt his heart swell as he felt her respond again. This was his woman, and he would take care of her.

"My duty as Lessa's guardian may take me dangerous places, Edie. I swear, next time I'll leave you in a safer place."

"No, Micha, no. I won't be left behind again. My place is at your side, and that's where I'll be." Edie pulled away and got up.

"Edie..." Micha scrambled to his feet and tried to embrace her again.

"No, this is not open for discussion." Edie held him at arm's length and searched his face. He couldn't seriously consider leaving her behind already.

"Edie, please. I couldn't bear it if anything happened to you."

"I belong at your side. Teach me to use weapons. I can learn to fight. You can't leave me behind to wait and worry. I don't think I could stand it again." Her eyes glistened but her resolve was firm. She loved this man dearly and would not be parted from him again.

"I see you're going to be as stubborn with me as I was with Lessa. Very well you shall have your way." Edie squealed and hugged him. "The crew could use a medic, and I hear that you're a good one."

Edie stepped back and searched his face. "I am, but I still need to learn to use weapons."

"You will not relent on this, will you?"

"I will not." Edie folded her arms across her chest and glared at him.

"Very well then, it'll be as you say." Micha smiled. He had himself a real firebrand. "Keira, are you still there?" There was a rustling of the grass then the heavily armed woman was with them. "Keira, this is my mate, Edie and she's precious to me. You must guard her well and teach her the ways of weapons and combat. Will you do this for me?"

Keira gave them a beautiful smile and patted his shoulder. She offered her hand to Edie and they grasped hands. "I'm Edie, Keira. Will you help me to be worthy of my mate?" Keira grinned and winked at her, then rose and vanished into the darkness. "Does she never speak, Micha?"

"She can't, Sweetheart. The Arlens cut out her tongue long ago."

"I suspect they did more than that. I swear I'll learn whatever she can teach."

"I know, but now I have another task for you." He sat back down and patted the ground beside him.

Edie crouched down. "Oh, really? Just what might that be?"

"For nearly two years I envisioned how sweet it would be to hold you while you slept. Now I want that dream to come true." He reached out to her and she settled down beside him.

"Is that all you envisioned?"

"No, but we did that already," he chuckled. "Now go to sleep." As Micha drifted off to sleep, Edie marveled at the fact she had accepted a warrior younger than herself and that he had returned a man of her own age. Truly these were magical times. Edie smiled one last time and succumbed to sleep.

Dawn broke to the sounds of gunfire. Micha was awake in a heartbeat, grasping at his clothes and weapons. He saw a number of soldiers on the hill, exchanging fire with Murtah. Brenna and Lessa raced down the hill as Keira charged up. Micha started up and Edie was instantly at his side. "Stay here, Edie."

"No, I'm going with you." Micha tore up the slope as he shouted to Edie. "Stay with Lessa! I'm not going anywhere. Lessa, make for the old mine site. We'll be right behind you."

He threw himself to the ground beside Keira and opened fire. With them laying down cover fire, Murtah was able to escape his hiding place in the boulders and join them. "We can hold them for a while, Micha, but they'll have reinforcements soon enough."

"I know. Murtah. It is time for a new plan." He fished in the pocket of his baggy trousers for a moment then came up with his communicator. "Zartah." No answer. "Zartah."

"Boss?"

"We're pinned down on the hillside and need a diversion."

"Aye, boss."

"Make it quick, Zurtah. Get ready everyone. They're coming."

Keira readied a flash tracer. A few moments later, two fighter ships streaked in low. As they neared Keira launched the tracer up the hill. A long wide ribbon of red smoke reached out towards the crest of the hill where the Arlen soldiers were taking cover behind the rocks. The ships altered course to attack.

They made a second pass then streaked away. When the soldiers looked out again, Micha and his crew were gone. Lessa, Brenna, and Edie were waiting by the largest building at the old mine site as Micha and companions came over the last hill and jogged down to meet them. Lessa raised her communicator. "Zartah, we're ready for pick up."

"Aye, Lady, incoming now." Micha barely had time to regain his breath before the two ships landed. They quickly climbed aboard and within minutes the ships were headed for Maccay territory.

The Maccay commander was waiting for them, accompanied by a tall, scowling man wearing a strange uniform, and a troop of armed men, all pointing weapons at them. "Boy, do you have any idea what you've done?"

Edie bristled at that, but Micha winked at her. Brenna spoke first. "Hello, Commander, it's good to see you so relieved that Edie and I've been reunited with our lovers and have escaped the Arlens."

"Brenna, I, well of course I'm glad you're unharmed, but you don't understand..."

"Enough! I'm General Dana of the Arcalian Alliance. I'm here to arrest you and deliver you to the Arlen Authority for your acts of Terrorism. Did you truly think you could impersonate the Arcalian Guard and get away with it? While we're at it, how did you manage to steal two of our finest fighting ships?"

"Long winded fellow isn't he?" chuckled Zartah, as he reached the ground.

"Indeed so. General, I'm Micha, friend of Lessa. I'm crew boss here. First, we weren't impersonating anyone; we just went in to get our people back."

"We didn't steal the ships either," chuckled Gorda as he alit from the fighter. "Your king gave them to me."

"You!"

"Yes me. I called in a favor. The boss needed ships. The king gave them to me, and I really don't think he'd be happy to learn you took them away."

"You have the ear and favor of the king, yet you would serve this child?"

"Any day of the week."

"You aren't arresting anyone either, General Dana. Take your troops and leave," said Lessa as she stepped forward.

"And just who do you think you are to be giving orders? The high priestess herself, perhaps?"

"Precisely," replied Lessa as she took off her scarf to show her tattoos. Everyone sank to their knees before her. "Micha, reveal the colors."

"Yes Ma'am." Micha pulled a patch off his uniform revealing a new patch beneath. It was a bright sunburst pattern in golds and red. The rest of his crew did the same. Gorda and Zartah peeled the cover off the new design on the ships. "Nova Prime," gasped the commander. "That sign is forbidden."

"That is the sign of my home world and my people. I now declare the ban on Nova Prime lifted. Novans may now wear these colors proudly once more. This man and his crew are my personal guards. They are not to be hindered in any way."

"The Viceroy will be pleased to know you have returned, Lady."

The general had a smirk on his face, but it disappeared quickly. "I give you leave to take the news to him, General. Tell him to prepare guest quarters. I will visit him soon. Go now, and take your men with you."

The general climbed to his feet, and with his troops in tow, retreated from the compound. His ship lifted off immediately. "He'll go straight to the Viceroy, Lady."

"I know he will, Commander, and that's what I wish him to do. Rise everyone. Return to your duties."

"Lessa, you revealed yourself."

"Yes, Brenna, I will no longer hide. I only stayed hidden until we had retrieved you. Had the Arlens learned of your connection to me and of my status, they'd have realized the power they held over me."

Lessa turned to the Arlen Commander. "Commander, you will provide tents and food for me and my retinue. Re-fuel our ships and restock the provisions and weapons. We'll leave in the morning."

"Yes Lady. It will be as you desire."

A moment later a soldier appeared to escort them to a large tent that had obviously been hastily vacated. There were bunks and a table of food. As they sat eating, Gorda was looking at Lessa, concern etched on his face."

"Gorda?"

"Lady, the general will go straight to the Viceroy. There'll be an armada waiting for us."

"Good, because we're going back to the farm before we go to the temple. It'll take a while for him to catch up and we will be ready for him when he does."

"We?"

"We have an ally, dear friends; a very powerful ally who is on Nova Prime right now. I ask you all to trust me in the days to come."

"You sound like you have a plan, Lessa," Micha observed.

"Yes I do, Micha, so everyone stop worrying. Brenna, what is it?"

"Lessa, ever since you told me of how Nova Prime was destroyed..."

"Yes?"

"Which company was it?" Brenna stood stiffly; her hands clasped together.

"R.I.M. Enterprises."

Tears sprang from Brenna's eyes as she absorbed that bit of information. Her hands rose to her breast as she struggled to speak. "My father was a new sector controller at that time. He was suddenly promoted to vice president, the youngest ever. No one ever spoke of it, but now I know why. That order would have had to come from him." Memories of all the lives she ended as a dispatcher suddenly came rushing back to her. One by one, the faces flashed through her mind. "Oh Lessa, what if I've become like him..." Brenna sank to the ground, sobbing.

"Hush now," soothed Lessa as she gathered Brenna into her arms.

"Lessa, I have killed over two hundred men, and..."

"Brenna, you committed no murders," said Edie as she knelt and cradled Brenna in her arms too. "Each life you took was done with compassion and the courage to look the man in the eye as you eased his pain. Your father struck from hiding like a coward. Your mother must be an amazing woman, and I'll bet it was from her you got your strength, courage and compassion."

Lessa was smiling and stroking Brenna's hair. "I'm sorry to be such a..."

"Hush now, Brenna," Edie said softly. "You've endured much, and now must release it. If this is how it must be done, we'll hold you each time until you're finally free of the pain."

"And the guilt..."

"You bear no guilt, Brenna. Had you not eased those men across the barrier, who knows how it might have been done, or if they would have been dumped out in the fields to die in pain, alone?"

"Thank you, Edie," sniffed Brenna. "As usual, you cut to the heart of the matter and put me back together." She reached up and touched her friend's face.

"You need to sleep, Brenna. Lady, can you help her to rest?"

"I can and will. Edie, you need to rest as well." Lessa reached out to stroke the hair back from Edie's eyes. "You've been a strong support for Brenna in my absence. I'm forever in your debt, my sister."

Edie blushed and returned to the cot beside Micha, who smiled at her proudly. She cuddled onto his shoulder and yawned. He laid her back and stretched out beside her.

She was asleep in moments. Micha smiled his thanks at Lessa and closed his eyes. Keira and Zartah played rock- paper-scissors, to see who would get the first watch. As usual, Zartah lost.

Return of the High Priestess

Next morning they found the ships prepared and provisioned. After a meal the commander presented Edie with a fresh med kit. "You might need this," he said as he passed it to her. "I have one for you too, Brenna."

"She will not need..."

"Thank you, my beloved, but I'll accept the gift. Thank you, Commander." Gorda climbed into one ship and the rest of them entered the other. There was just enough room for all to be comfortable. "Gorda, take no chances; do what you must and no more."

"Aye boss." Gorda grinned as he switched off the communicator. Both ships rose from the ground and leaped towards space. The Arlen guns opened fire and one ship turned to do battle. One fast strafing run and Gorda swung back out into space. Several Arlen ships gave chase, and several more were following the first ship. Gorda shot down two before he pulled alongside the second ship. Both suddenly leaped to full burn and were away.

No ship in the Arlen fleet could hope to catch them at full burn. They all turned back. "Have we lost pursuit?" Micha inquired.

"Nothing on sensors."

"Good." Micha took the communicator in hand. "Well done, Gorda. Course change coming up."

"We're not going to visit the Viceroy after all?"

"Not just yet. We're going back to the farm. Lock ships first so we can spread out a bit." The two ships moved together, the locks extended, clamped, and the air lock sealed. Micha, Edie, and Keira moved over to Gorda's craft then the ships separated. Five days later they were landing at the farm.

"Damn, I seriously wish we had a freighter big enough to put both ships in and let us stretch out a bit," grumbled Zartah as they reached the ground.

"Good idea," said Micha as he stretched the kinks out of his back. "Take whatever is left of the crew's script plus all of mine. After you get something to eat, see what you can do for fuel and passage, would you, Gorda?"

"Aye boss."

Next morning, they enjoyed the morning meal with the other settlers in Murtah's group. These were good people and he would miss them all. Murtah sat back and sighed before speaking. "Amon, this farm is yours now. Ena will leave with me when the ship returns for us."

"Murtah, are you certain? This is good land and a safe planet."

"I know, Amon, and you'll prosper here. There is somewhere I must go, and I want Ena with me. We'll come for the children when it's safe to do so."

"They can stay here as long as they like, Murtah, you know that. I'll keep them safe for you."

"Thank you, Amon, you're a good friend."

"Where are we going, my husband?" Ena asked.

"There is a place where we can farm. It's good land and they'll need many farmers there, as well as warriors. Zartah's going and so I would go there as well. Once we're settled we'll send for the children."

"You can tell them our destination, Murtah. It's no longer secret."

"Thank you, Lady. We're going to Nova Prime."

There was a collective intake of breath at that. "You'll die..."

"The atmosphere has been cleared," said Lessa. "We'll gather all Novans to us and rebuild Nova."

"Lady, this could bring the return of the companies, it could start a galactic war."

"My entire race was once slaughtered, but now there is a chance to rebuild what was lost. I will not cower and do nothing!" Everyone shrank from the sudden fury in Lessa's face. She was on her feet pacing about the room. "I will offer no affront to the companies, or any other, but I will rebuild Nova, and may the fates have mercy on any who try to cross my path."

There was an aura of darkness and danger gathering around her and she trembled with the emotions that gripped her. Micha rose and approached her. "Lessa, have some more tea."

"Micha, I need no tea..."

"Here, drink this." He handed her a mug of strong tea. "Lessa, these folk aren't the enemy; they're just afraid. Don't be a cross patch, drink some tea. Let us go and leave them in peace. We'll rebuild Nova, and I'll do battle with any and all who come to get in our way. I won't let anyone stop us; I swear it."

Lessa looked at the others, still holding their breath, and then turned to the one man in the room with courage to face her anger. Suddenly grateful for her friend's intervention, she smiled at Micha, accepted the mug and took a sip. "If you call me a cross patch again, I'll turn you into a toad."

"Noted," he grinned as he stepped back from her.

"Forgive me, my friends. Micha is right, I do need more tea. This planet is far from Nova, so, should the worst happen, you will still be safe here. I will not bring destruction down upon you. I've blessed this land and I truly want to see this farm prosper. As soon as Gorda returns we'll take our troubles elsewhere."

She smiled once more before turning on her heel and leaving the building. Brenna was close behind her and found her with tears in her eyes. "What does it take, Brenna? How much evil can be done and not one soul have the courage to stand up and say stop. Do what you will to others, just don't notice me. That's their only thought."

"Easy, Lessa my darling. They mean us no harm, but they're farmers, not warriors."

"I know. I just grow impatient to get this done and take you to our new home."

"Get what done, lover?"

"We will put a stop to this high priestess marriage abuse thing and restore the true power of the high priestess. After that we'll take the suppressors off every woman in his harem. We'll bring down the Viceroy. Finally, we'll bring down the council of the Holy Temple and re-establish a proper system of administration."

"When you say 'we', do you mean the nine of us?"

"Brenna, we have an ally of incredible power. My love, you know I wouldn't risk you. Be assured, this will happen."

"I trust you. You haven't failed me yet."

"You no longer fear me and my mad schemes?"

"No, I've found my courage. I've chosen you and we'll face our fates together, whatever they may be."

"Thank you, sweetheart." Lessa's eyes wandered down to the dispatcher's kit hanging from Brenna's belt. "Why did you accept the dispatcher's kit again? You have no need of that now, and after what happened a while back..."

"It's part of who I am now, Lessa. I was once a teacher and a believer in the system, young and naive. I'm now a dispatcher, simply trying to assist the dying to pass with dignity. It's difficult at times. I'm far from comfortable with it, but I am happy to be so, given my father's comfort with taking life. Still, it's taught me much about life and about myself."

"I would make you a teacher again, Brenna."

"Perhaps I can be both. Look, there's a ship coming now." Micha came blasting out the door, bawling orders. "Zartah, get that ship warmed up. Murtah, Ena, get in there with him. Everybody else into Gorda's ship."

Gorda was dropping the hatch open even before the ship touched down. They clambered aboard as quickly as possible, Edie hauling

Micha in as the ship rose in the air. "Keira, man the guns! Boss we've got trouble!"

"I've got the tail gun. Give Zartah some cover if he needs it."

"He'll need it. The man is still on the ground."

Five small fighters dropped in out of the rising sun and opened fire. Gorda evaded and Keira returned fire. As the fighters swept past, she brought down one and Micha got another from the tail gun turret. The three remaining fighters banked tightly and were on their trail in an instant.

"Hang on," bawled Gorda, as he suddenly reversed engines and dropped beneath the pursuers. He came back up behind them and Keira got two more. Then the last fighter took a missile from behind and exploded. Zartah had joined the battle. "Clear."

"Clear here," squawked the communicator. "See, Gorda, I told you. There's always something exciting to do on this crew."

"That was a bit too exciting, Zartah. Those Arlen fighters came in on a merc transport. They've been tracking us. We're going to comb these two ships until we find how they did it. Follow me folks. We're riding in style this time." He headed straight out into space. Soon their ships passed the planet's third moon. That's when they saw the big freighter.

Gorda flew straight at the freighter which opened a welcoming cargo door. Both ships landed easily inside and the door closed. A communicator came to life. "Atmosphere re-established. Welcome aboard the Albatross." It was a woman's voice. As they climbed down from the fighters a woman was waiting for them.

Micha recognized her. "Kella, right?"

"Right, Micha. Remember that I once told you I had friends in strange places? Well one of them has a smuggling business that works the war zones. Dangerous work, for sure, but the pay is great. I work for him now, and this is my ship. I told him I had to borrow it for a while."

"He doesn't mind?"

"No, Father doesn't mind," she grinned. "Come on, I'll show you around the ship." Micha introduced everyone as Kella led them out of the cargo hold. Gorda and Keira stayed behind to search for the tracking device that had nearly been the end of them.

"So, how do you know Micha?" asked Edie as they entered the spacious eating galley.

"You must be Edie. We heard all about you, many times." Kella smiled. "Micha took several of us out of a prison where we were condemned to death. He saved me and restored me to my family. Now I get to repay the kindness."

Micha's communicator crackled. "Boss, we found and disabled two tracking devices."

"Where did you find them?"

"One in the med kit and the other in the dispatcher's kit. Looks like the Maccay commander was on the Arlen payroll."

"Understood. Come on up."

Edie looked at Micha quizzically. "You talked about me to strangers?"

"He talked about you to anyone who would listen," grinned Kella. "You've got the poor boy bewitched."

"Indeed, that's good to know. I intend to keep him that way." Edie winked at her lover. Micha blushed and turned away to carefully inspect the walls.

"Lady, now that the tracking devices have been disabled, we can get under way. May I have a destination?" Kella inquired.

"You know who I am?" Lessa spoke as if it was a statement of fact rather than a question.

"Yes, Lady," replied the woman as she sank to one knee. "Surely the guardian of the high priestess wouldn't be far from her."

"Very astute, Kella, friend of Micha. Rise, girl, this isn't the temple, but that's where I wish to go with all due haste."

"The temple on Borealis Prime?"

"You'd prefer not to return there, I know. I promise they won't get their hands on you again."

"Thank you, Lady, I do appreciate that. Very well then, let's get under way." Kella grabbed her communicator. "Elkin, Borealis Prime, maximum burn."

"Aye captain, Borealis Prime, Maximum burn."

That night Brenna slept in a fresh bed, snuggled in Lessa's arms, something she had dreamed often during her two years of hell. In the midst of chaos, near total exhaustion, Brenna would fall into a deep sleep where she would dream of Lessa. The dreams had been so real that she often felt the soft kiss of Lessa's lips and the gentle warmth of her embrace. The dreams had been more real to her than the war outside her hut.

Those dreams had been all that kept her going at times, and now they had come to pass. She snuggled closer, tears of joy and release leaking from her eyes. Edie lay beside Micha, their passion just spent, marveling at the newfound sweetness of her life. The waiting was over; Micha had come for her, just as he'd promised to do.

They'd left his sister, Alla, back on the farm as there was a young fellow there with whom she would not part. Edie had Micha's full attention whenever they were alone, and she blossomed in it. The journey gave the entire crew a much-needed break.

For two weeks they relaxed and made plans in the relative luxury of the large ship. Part of each day was devoted to hand-to-hand combat practice under Murtah's guidance. Lessa enhanced each and every one of them to their maximum ability. She wanted her guard to survive if things went badly, and she gave them the means to do so.

On the third week they entered Borelian space. The local authorities contacted them almost immediately. Kella gave them her story, sent the appropriate codes and they were allowed to continue.

"Security has been heightened since your last visit two years ago, Lady."

"So I see. Will your story be sufficient?"

"It'll get us close, but the nearer we get to Borealis Prime, the tighter the security gets, or so I've been told. I confess I've stayed well out of Borelian Space since our escape from the temple prison."

"I will not put you back in their field of interest, Kella. May I touch you?"

"Of course, Lady." Lessa cradled the woman's face in her hands for a moment. Kella felt a tingling sensation. As Lessa removed her hands, the others gasped in delight. Kella looked like a much younger version of herself. This young woman could not possibly be the one who escaped two years past.

Kella retrieved a small mirror and touched her face. She could hardly believe it was her own reflection. "It'll wear off in a month or two, but for now, you're a young girl again." Lessa smiled as Kella traced the shape of her own face with questing fingers. "Some may think they recognize your face, Kella, but you're obviously far too young to be the escaped convict. You'll be quite safe in Borelian space."

"Lady, thank you. Oh gods, I can't believe this." She was now inspecting her new face in the reflection of a window. At length she turned around and spoke, smiling. "Since I'm far too young to captain a ship, Elkin, for the next while you're captain and I'm your daughter, Keeta."

"Go to your cabin, Keeta," chuckled Elkin, "the bridge is no place for a child."

"The gods will punish you for that, Elkin, and so will I." She poked him in the ribs and walked away. Kella returned to her cabin to fully inspect her face in the mirror. After a long look she suddenly squealed in glee and danced around for a moment.

"I risked much to repay my debt to Micha, but now I see there's more here. He said the Lady protects her friends, and I see the truth of that. I must prove worthy of her kindness, for I sense great change in the worlds. As Father always says, if you must choose a side, choose the right one."

She smiled as she lay back on her bunk and took up her reading tablet. Two days later they were approaching Borealis Prime once again. As the war ship appeared, demanding access to the ship, Lessa stepped before the vid screen. "Silence, put your captain on coms, now."

"At once, Lady." A moment later the captain appeared on the screen and sank to one knee as Lessa spoke again.

"Send a shuttle for me, our intership lock is damaged."

"At once, Lady." He struggled to his feet, but she had already broken the connection. "All right, here we go. Are we all ready?"

"Ready, Lessa." Micha was adjusting his weapons. He lightly kissed Edie then hugged her tightly. "Are you sure you're ready for this?"

"I'm as ready as can be, Micha. Lessa has enhanced my abilities as she did yours, I won't disappoint you."

"That never crossed my mind," he said smiling at her and then turning back to Lessa. "All right, we're ready."

"Shuttle docking."

"Let's go." Lessa had donned official robes, and with Micha and Edie as guards, strode regally to the shuttle and entered. The pilot remained silent as he took them to the big ship. Once on board Lessa headed for the bridge. The captain met her halfway and sank to one knee, but she walked right past him. She entered the bridge with him close behind her. "Get me to the temple, all possible speed."

"Aye, Lady." The ship turned and leaped away, the old freighter following at a much slower rate. Lessa paced the deck as the ship sped towards the planet. As they neared, they were challenged by ground control. "BSS Raptor, why have you abandoned your station? All stop until..."

"Be silent," snapped Lessa as she stepped in front of the vid screen. "Clear a path to the temple for this ship. Quickly."

"Yes, Lady, at once, Lady..." he was babbling to thin air as Lessa had already cut the connection. The ship continued unhindered to the landing pad of the high priestess. As the big ship settled to the ground and lowered the boarding ramp, Salian and the council were waiting.

Lessa descended from the ship, flanked by two heavily armed guards. "Not this time, Arlessa, by order of the Council I..." Salian's voice failed her as Lessa held out her hand. Salian and the entire council were forced to their knees by a power they could not have imagined existed. Arlessa could defeat any one or two of them, but all five plus the regent was unbelievable.

She strode past with her two armed guards at her side. "Attend me." As she spoke, the spell was broken and they were released. Rising swiftly, they hurried along behind her. Striding down the main hallway Lessa spotted a young priestess flattening herself against the wall, trying to stay out of the way.

"You there."

"Lady?"

"Sound the bells, call the assembly. Quickly."

"Yes Lady." The girl scurried away and a moment later bells sounded throughout the temple. Lessa entered the great hall and climbed to the raised dais where she took her high seat. The benches soon began to fill up as women hurried through every entrance. When all the seats were filled and no more seemed to be coming, she rose to speak. Her voice was strong and easily reached those people far to the rear.

"I am Arlessa of Nara, high priestess of Borealis Solaris Temple, and all regions of this sector of space. I come before this assembly today to deal justice and to proclaim Temple law." There was a murmur at this.

"First of the accused is Salian, former Regent of the Temple." There was a collective gasp from the throng as all eyes turned to the red-faced accused. "Two years ago she tried to capture and disable me. She failed. Polina, step forward." Nothing happened except a nervous shuffling in the seats.

"She is not here, Lady, she will be in the kitchens." came a soft hesitant voice from the front row of benches.

"Bring her to me now."

The young one was up and gone in a heartbeat. No one moved or spoke while they waited. The young priestess soon returned with an older woman in tow. She resumed her seat as the woman knelt before Lessa.

"Rise, Polina, and tell me why you were in the kitchens dressed as a pot scrubber while an assembly is in progress."

"Lady, only a priestess, or those in training, may attend the assembly. I am neither."

"You're the finest instructor this temple has, Polina. Who reduced you to kitchen staff?"

"The Regent, Lady."

"Indeed. Salian, your punishment for your treason is to exchange positions with Polina. She is now the Regent; you are reduced to kitchen staff. Remove your robe of office and pass it to Polina, then get yourself to the kitchen." Trembling with impotent rage, Salian began to remove her robe.

Suddenly she hurled a fireball at Lessa, but it fizzled out in midair. Lessa leaned forward and spoke in a cold dangerous voice. "Very well. Since you've rejected the kitchens, you've chosen the prisons instead. Remove her." She watched dispassionately as Salian was fitted with an inhibitor then led away.

Lessa wasn't finished. "Members of the council, stand." They did. "That which was hidden from me was found. I've spent the past two years studying in that library. I've also removed it to a safe place; one where you cannot find it. Since you plotted against me with Salian and the Viceroy, I depose you. Remove your chains of office and leave this place or you will suffer the same fate as Salian."

"The Viceroy will come for you, Arlessa. Even you cannot defeat the might of his armies!" declared the eldest of the councillors, her aged voice trembling as she shook an accusing finger at Lessa.

"Ah yes, my husband to be. It is precisely to attract his attention that I've returned at this time. Remove your chains of office or perish where you stand!"

Lessa rose to her feet, her eyes flashing fire and magic fire dancing in her hands. One by one they removed the chains of office, passed them to Polina, and then hurried from the hall.

"Polina, appoint a new ruling council as quickly as possible." Lessa resumed her high seat.

"Yes, Lady, and may I express my joy at your return. Lady, there are people in the prisons who deserve to be on the council."

"Of course, Regent. Release who you will with my blessing. First, bring forth the book of laws and a scribe." Polina addressed a priestess in training and sent her to fetch the scribe. Within minutes both the scribe and the book were in front of Lessa. Only the high priestess or the council could open the book, and Lessa was quick to do so.

She signaled the scribe forward. As soon as the woman was ready, she spoke again. "Article one. Henceforth, the high priestess will have the freedom of choice in marriage. She is free to marry, or not, anyone she chooses. She is also free to hold the office of High Priestess as long as the council deems her able. I, Arlessa, High Priestess, declare it so."

She signed the article and Polina witnessed it before the assembly. "Article two. Henceforth, no man will place an inhibitor upon his mate for any reason." Again she signed and Polina, as Regent, witnessed.

"I will now retire to my office. Scribe, have food and water brought there for myself and my guardians. Polina, attend me."

"Yes Lady!" The scribe rose and gave orders. "Prepare the Lady's chambers for herself and her companions." People scattered in all directions as they left the assembly hall.

They marched into a side corridor which took them to the private offices of the high priestess. Everything was spotlessly clean and the place looked well used. It should have been sealed up for many years, but it hadn't.

"Salian used this office," Polina said as they entered. "I foolishly chastised her for her presumption and was demoted to the kitchens for my efforts."

"I see. Polina, I give you permission to use my offices whenever you wish."

"Thank you, Arlessa. We should begin to prepare our defenses now; much good it will do us in the end."

"Do not fear the Viceroy, old friend. His end is near. There'll be no defense necessary except me and my allies."

"So you did find the library! No matter, Arlessa; even the Black Witch herself couldn't defeat the Viceroy and his armada. He has grown strong in the use of power himself and his armada is well equipped."

"You think not?" smiled Lessa. "Well, we'll soon see, she'll be arriving shortly." Polina gulped but didn't speak. Her widened eyes spoke of her fear. "Oh yes, Norlene is here in this time period, and I've sent for her. Soon you will meet the Black Witch of legend."

Micha startled to the news that the Black Witch was on her way. "You didn't need me here, Lessa, Edie and I should have gone with the others."

"But I did need you, Micha. The sight of you and Edie gave everyone pause. Some might have attacked had I been alone, then I'd have been forced to kill them. Your presence here saved many lives this day. I know you're worried about the others, but they're stronger than we realize, you know this is true."

"It is true," Edie replied. "Miss O'Loran is so different now than when we first met, so much stronger. And whatever she can't handle, Keira will certainly shoot. So, what do we do now?"

"Now we wait for the Viceroy to call and hope that our allies have been successful."

"Have you got a backup plan, Lessa?"

"I always have one, Micha, but I truly don't want to use it this time."

"Then let's hope Miss O'Loran is successful."

Gathering Allies

As the warship sank through the atmosphere to deliver Lessa and her escort to the temple, the two fighter ships dropped out of the freighter and split off. One swept close to the ground and went north while the other headed off into space at full burn. Ground control didn't question either ship as Lessa had forbidden it. The power struggle between Lessa and the Viceroy was now about to be settled and nobody wanted to get in the middle or declare sides.

The ship heading out into space carried only the pilot, the other a compliment of five. It headed north into the territory of the Nara Clan. The ship landed easily only to be surrounded by armed troops. A man spoke through the communicator. "Come out with your hands in the air, Arcalians."

"I'm not a bloody Arcalian, you idiot, I'm Zartah, Korath's son, of Nara Clan."

"Show your marks." He did so and the armed men lowered their weapons slightly. "Come out and state your business." He stood back as the hatch swung open and two men dropped to the ground. They looked enough alike to be brothers. As soon as they were clear, the ship rose again and shot out into space.

The man in command stepped forward then stopped. "Murtah, is that you?"

"It is. Eamon, isn't it? It's been a long time. This is my brother Zartah."

"Too long, my old teacher. You should not be here, either of you. No doubt there's a reward on both your heads. Troop dismissed; I'll deal with this personally. Come, we will talk in my office."

They followed him inside where he flopped into a chair behind a battered desk, indicating they should sit. "All right, Murtah, I'll help you as best I can. What's brought you back now, and what do you need, besides fast transport out of here?"

"We need an audience with the chieftain, and we need it today, tomorrow at the latest."

"You must be out of your mind. I couldn't arrange that in a month. He's a very busy man and he doesn't see a lot of people, if you know what I mean."

"Just tell him you have me in custody. That should do it." Zartah smiled.

"All right, if that's how you want it." Eamon turned and spoke into to his communicator. A few moments later he turned back to them. "You have an appointment first thing tomorrow. I'm to put you in guest quarters. Everything you need will be provided for you, and a guide will come for you in the morning. Murtah, perhaps you should have stayed with the ship, out of sight."

"He stays with me. Murtah's my brother and was falsely accused. We've come to set things straight."

"As you wish, I'll have a transport and driver assigned to you immediately."

A few moments later a transport arrived. They were whisked away to guest quarters near the Chieftain's mansion. Beds were prepared for them as well as hot baths and a large table of food. Murtah paced and fumed while Zartah settled in to wait. Eventually Murtah tired and sat facing the door.

Despite the plushness of their surroundings, both men were far from relaxed. Murtah was awake early. Zartah eyes opened the second Murtah's feet hit the floor; both men were ready to go long before their guide arrived. She led them to a large waiting room then left them on their own.

Murtah circled the room many times before they were shown into the chieftain's office. Zartah tried to convince him that this was just a negotiation tactic and they just had to play it out. It didn't help; Murtah still paced.

"I see you still haven't learned to sit still, Murtah," grinned a tall man as he entered the room. "Come into my office, men." They entered and he indicated they should sit. "Now, tell me why the hell you're here with me risking capture and death."

"I'm here on behalf of Arlessa, High Priestess of the Temple." His laughter was full and rich. "All right, Murtah, I've heard that you joined up with her, and that Nova patch on your jacket confirms it. So, how can I be of service to the high priestess?"

"She wants you to be the next Viceroy, Lortax." The smile left their host's face in favor of surprise.

"Viceroy? Has she gone completely mad? That office is filled by a man I do not wish to challenge."

"Aye," grinned Murtah, "for the moment."

"What do you mean?"

"Lady Arlessa is about to remove him from office, permanently."

"Even the greatest witch alive can't stand against that armada. No, Murtah, this is madness."

"The Lady has an ally, Lortax," chuckled Zartah, "a very powerful ally."

"Who in the right mind would face the Viceroy?"

"The Black Witch herself." Zartah grinned.

"Gah, you two have lost your minds!"

"It's true, Lortax," Murtah said seriously. "The Black Witch Norlene has leaped through time to help Arlessa. She's already cleared the atmosphere of Nova Prime so we can return there."

"She's done what?" Lortax searched both men's faces for a moment before speaking again. "You do speak the truth, don't you?"

"I swear, Lortax, I'd never speak of Nova Prime in jest. The Black Witch is coming, the viceroy will fall, and the entire sector will crumble into chaos unless someone with a strong hand rises to take control. The Lady will make you Viceroy, you'll have the backing of the Temple, and with that the clans will rise with you. The chance to return Nara Clan to her rightful place is at hand, Lortax."

"You're certain of all you have told me?"

"Here is Lady Arlessa'a ring as proof of my words," Murtah said. Lortax looked at the ring in his hand and sighed. "All right then, go back to your quarters and tell the Lady I'm coming."

He'd been reluctant at first, but Murtah was skilled at negotiations and, in the end he had the commitment he wanted. They returned to guest quarters to wait. Back in his office the chieftain was bawling orders and mobilizing his forces.

———⊶◉⊷———

AS SOON AS KEIRA DROPPED the brothers off at clan headquarters, she sent the ship hurtling back into space. This was going to be a hard mission and it was her responsibility to keep Brenna and Ena safe. There were more things that could go wrong than she cared to count. Had anyone but the high priestess asked her to do it she would probably have refused.

Ah well, too late now, she was already closing on Borealis Two, home world of the Viceroy. As they drew near the planet, Brenna donned the black hood dispatchers sometimes wore on formal occasions. When Ground Control challenged them, Brenna stepped before the vid screen. "I am the dispatcher assigned to attend the ladies of the harem."

"Dispatcher? No one told me a dispatcher had been summoned. We have our own people here who can take care of the harems needs."

"I am so sorry your Viceroy didn't see fit to consult you in the running of his household. It surely would have saved me a trip.

However, I'm here to work. Send me away if you wish and you can explain it to His Excellency yourself."

The man on the vid screen disappeared for a moment. When he returned, his face was pale. "You may land outside the palace. Prepare for inspection."

"Thank you," replied Brenna evenly. "I'm sure the Viceroy will be pleased you agree with his summons."

Keira brought the ship down gracefully. The hatch opened and three women dropped to the ground, one hooded with a well-worn dispatch kit, one with a med kit and wearing the red and white arm band of a battlefield medic, and one heavily armed female warrior. Several armed men strode up to them.

"Drop all your weapons."

"She will not. This woman is our medic; she'll determine if the dispatch is truly required, if so I will perform the duty, and my bodyguard will make certain no one tries to interfere. She retains her arms. Now, fetch transportation, I want to get this done; we're needed back at the front."

The man in command had no idea why a battlefield dispatcher had arrived, but the Viceroy had dispatched more than one over the years. He knew better than to question. In mere moments they were transported to the north wing of the palace and ushered in to the harem.

Brenna swallowed hard and tried not to show emotion. There were over a dozen women, all gazing blankly out the window. They showed no real interest in the newcomers at all. "Come here to me, one at a time," said Ena, who was wearing Edie's medic armband. Obediently, the women turned away from the window and formed a line. Keira guarded the door as Brenna and Ena removed the inhibitors one by one. As each woman was freed of the mental shackles, she began to recall her past life. Five of these women had been high priestess at one time.

As soon as all were freed, Brenna explained what had happened to them, and that it would take a day or two for their memories to fully return.

"Arlessa is high priestess now? She was only a girl yesterday."

"That was many years ago."

"Years? Yes, I suppose it could have been years since I made the sacrifice."

"The sacrifice?"

"Yes, it is how the temple retains the magic. Every three years the high priestess marries the Viceroy and accepts the inhibitor. Her successor reigns for three years then she too makes the sacrifice. If the sacrifice is not made each three years, the magic will fade forever."

"It was all a lie," said Brenna gently. "Arlessa has escaped the sacrifice for years and has only grown stronger in her magic. Wait until you meet her, you'll see the truth of this. The sacrifice is just a way for the Viceroy and the Regent to keep the political power. We'll take you all back to the temple where you'll see for yourselves."

"We'll need a bigger ship, Brenna," said Ena. "We can't fit everyone into the fighter."

"I will help you with this," declared the woman who had remembered Lessa as a girl. "My name is Marla, and I was high priestess once. I think I can still wield some power, and perhaps a bit of influence. Come, let's go."

As they opened the door to leave the two guards raised their weapons to prevent them. Keira struck with blinding speed and both men were on the floor, unconscious. She'd hardly made a sound. They strode into the main hall and servants suddenly appeared, then, shocked, tried to slip away.

Marla quickly took control. "You there, fetch the Viceroy's secretary. Quickly now." The woman sped away and soon returned with a small balding man in tow. "We need a transport ship, now. Have one sent here to the palace grounds."

"Madam, I don't believe the Viceroy would approve..."

"I care not of what he approves," said Marla as she formed a small fireball in her hand. "Do as I bid you, or I'll fry you for dinner."

"Yes Ma'am," he gulped as he fumbled for a communicator. An hour later the transport arrived. Keira returned to her own ship and blasted off as escort for the small passenger transport. They rose into space then headed for Borealis Prime. When they arrived, the passenger ship went straight to the temple, but Keira swung north to rejoin the brothers.

———◉———

AS GORDA SPED AWAY on his lonely mission, he seriously thought about turning and heading straight out into space. Maybe he could hide out on that farm planet in the Maccay System. Then again, how could you hide from someone like Arlessa? Besides, he liked and trusted her.

Then there was his allegiance to Micha. How that boy, still in his teens, could inspire such loyalty was a mystery. No, he could not let Micha down. This task was truly going to tax his ability to trust and believe. Ah well, perhaps he could survive it. It had been many years since the plague ravaged Nova Prime. Perhaps the air was safe to breathe.

He continued his rumination during the whole trip. Many long hours later he saw Nova Prime on the screen, a small ball of light in the distance, but it was growing closer. When it began to fill the screen he sent the message Lessa had given him. A moment later there was a landing beacon transmitting from the planet below. He flew in over empty cities, abandoned mines, and empty farms. Nothing moved anywhere.

Arriving at the beacon, he set the ship down gently then disembarked. A woman dressed in flowing black robes was approaching and he dropped to one knee before her. "Lady."

"Rise, are you a messenger from Arlessa?"

"Yes, Lady. I'm Gorda, specialist of Micha's crew, in service to Arlessa, High Priestess of the Temple."

"Perhaps I should just call you Gorda. Your title would be tiring to speak." Norlene smiled as she gracefully lowered herself to the ground. "Come, Gorda, sit here beside me and give me the news."

He relayed his news, as respectfully as he could manage, but in the end, his curiosity got the better of him. "Lady, are you truly the Black Witch?"

"Ha, that and more! I'm Norlene, High Priestess of the Temple, Holder of the Sacred Chalice, Guardian of the Library of True Knowledge, and a number of other silly things that make no difference at all. Yes, Gorda, I'm the one your mother probably threatened you with; however, I've never eaten a child, nor will I. How in the heavens did this foolishness get started?"

"Perhaps the color of your robes?"

"These? I was in mourning, for pity sake. My beloved Meka was barely cold in the ground when Arlessa came barging into the library, demanding I teach her everything, jumping about like an excited puppy through the timelines, creating more havoc than you can imagine. So I took her between times and taught her what I could. She's become far more powerful than even I. The girl truly has a gift for the magic. So, what else do you know of me?"

"It's said that, in your grief, you tried to bring your lover back from the dead, and that the evil of the spell consumed you."

"Fools, idiots, nincompoops! Ah well, perhaps the legend may be of some help to us in the coming days. Let's go, Gorda. We can be of more use at the temple. I've done all I can do here."

"Lady, this planet is supposed to be plague ridden, how did you cleanse it?"

"When I arrived, the air was unfit, and the land littered with the rotted bodies of men, women, children, and beasts. Nothing lived.

I destroyed the bodies and used the energy release to cleanse the atmosphere. The air is sweet and my people are at rest now. We'll rebuild Nova, but first we have a Viceroy to deal with, I believe.

"Come, Gorda, hoist me into that contraption and get me to the temple. Arlessa is waiting, and she can be impatient."

He didn't need to hoist her anywhere, for Norlene pulled herself into the fighter with ease. She grinned at him then readjusted her robes as he settled into the pilot's seat. The ship lifted off gracefully then blasted into space.

Halfway to Borealis Prime every alarm in the ship sounded, waking them both. The weapons had automatically come online and powered up.

Showdown

One glance at the screen and Gorda started swearing. "Grab on to something." He threw the ship into a hard bank at full burn then readjusted his trajectory and hit the super accelerator. It only lasted a moment, used up half their fuel, but it put them well out in front of the armada that they had nearly crashed into.

"Nicely done," smiled Norlene, "but I could have handled that." "
Sorry. I just reacted. Don't want to get lazy."

"Lazy?"

"Micha, Arlessa's guardian and my crew boss, says working for a witch can make you lazy if you depend on her to magic everything. The crew never asks Lessa for help and she only offers when all else has failed."

"I think I'm going to like your crew boss, Gorda. Perhaps we should let them catch us, though. I might be able to slow them down a bit. It would give Arlessa more time to prepare."

"She told me to get you to the temple as fast as possible. I'll stop, but you'll have to protect me from the boss when he finds out I let the armada have you."

She chuckled and then indicated he should stop the ship. Gorda reversed engines and let the armada overtake him. A ship soon clamped on and an air lock was extended. Men pounded on the air lock door, but it wouldn't open. The communicator leaped to life. "Open that damned hatch, in the name of the Viceroy, I command it."

"In the name of Norlene, the Black Witch of Nova Prime, I refuse." Gorda grinned widely as he replied.

"Bloody fool, I'll blast your ship halfway to the Galactic core if you..." Norlene stepped in front of the vid screen and held up her hand.

The man instantly grasped at his own throat and struggled for breath, breath he could not get.

"I find your attitude annoying," she said, in a voice as cold as deep space. She opened her hand and released him. She gave him a moment to regain his breath then she spoke again. "If this armada has a flagship, bring it here at once. I do not parley with minions." She made a motion with her hand and Gorda cut the connection.

"There now, that should do it," she grinned. "They'll fuss for a while, then some idiot will come posturing, I'll embarrass him, then the Viceroy will come. We'll see what'll happen from there. In the meantime, we seem to have brought the armada to a halt. Not bad for two people in a single ship."

She was grinning and Gorda was shaking his head. He was starting to like her a lot. A larger ship soon appeared. "We will escort you to the Viceroy's ship. Do not deviate from the course we set for you."

Norlene was at the screen in a heartbeat. The man was suddenly writhing in pain on the deck of his ship and another face appeared. "I said to bring the flagship to me here. Send another minion and I'll start obliterating ships. Now go."

"That should get his attention, Lady. May I ask why it is so important for him to come here instead of us going to his ship?"

"It's a stalling tactic, Gorda, but it'll also put him in a defensive position. He's been summoned by a high priestess. This embarrassed him before his whole armada. He will now attempt to gain the upper hand. Do you know anything of this man?"

"I know he's used to getting whatever he wants, he can wield power as well as any witch, and, according to rumor, he's a right bastard."

"Good to know," she chuckled, "good to know. Here comes the bastard now. Let's see what he's made of."

A moment later a huge warship swung alongside. The coms came to life and an older man with an oily smile appeared on the screen. "I hear the Black Witch of Borealis is aboard your ship. I am the Viceroy and I've come to beg an audience. Your fighter is a bit cramped for my taste. Perhaps we could meet here on my ship? I'll be happy to provide refreshments."

"Accepted," replied Norlene. "Send your escort. My pilot will remain aboard the fighter."

"As you desire, Lady. Your escort will meet you at the air lock."

"Lady, are you certain of this?"

"Trust me, Gorda, I can handle this. Just play along until we get to the temple. I'm going to mess with this man's mind a bit. It should be fun, the arrogant bugger." Gorda chuckled as she headed for the air lock. The escort turned out to be four armed guards.

Norlene smiled to herself as she marched along with two before her and two behind. At length they arrived at a large meeting room where she was instructed to sit. Instead, she began to pace around, inspecting the walls of the room. "See anything interesting?" asked the Viceroy as he entered the room.

"Just looking for the weak spots, you know, in case we start throwing power around. We don't want to rupture the hull while we're playing, now do we?"

"So, you're the legendary Black Witch."

"Was that a question or a statement?"

"I don't know what you game is, woman, but I'm not amused. You've managed to stop my entire fleet with a few parlor tricks that any apprentice could manage. Just what is your game?"

"My game?"

"What do you want?"

"Information. I'm a curious woman, I like to know things."

"What sort of things do you want to know?"

"All sorts of things. For example, as far as I know, the wars are far from Borealis space, yet here you are with a fresh armada, ready for battle. Have the clans arisen against the ruling class?"

"I'll tell you what I'd like to know. I'd like to know who in the nine hells of Porapix you actually are, who sent you, and just what you hope to accomplish."

"All right, an exchange of information it is. You go first." Suddenly Norlene was hurled against the wall and held there, several feet from the floor, by a crushing weight. "I tire of this foolishness, woman. Now speak or die."

Norlene smiled as she easily floated to the floor, even though he poured on more power. She pushed his power back at him as she stepped toward him. "If we toss around enough power we'll tear this pretty ship apart. I suggest we go back to the exchange of information."

"Who are you?" he asked as he relented and sank into a plush chair.

"I'm Norlene, the Black Witch. Your turn now. Where're you going with a war fleet?"

"We go to Borealis Prime. The Black Witch perished generations ago. How did you get here?"

"I time shifted to this time. Damned near killed me too; that was a big jump. So, what's happening on Borealis Prime that requires the Viceroy to bring his armada?"

"I'm trying to pin down a criminal who has evaded us for years. Where were you going when we stopped you?"

"Criminal eh? I was on my way to Borealis Prime, to the temple. Actually, my pilot outran your fleet, but I asked him to wait for you."

"Why?"

"Safety in numbers, I feel a lot safer in the company of your fleet than on my own."

"Really? Then why did you make such a fuss about talking to me personally?"

"I wanted to meet you, of course. Ah, I see we're under way again."

"Indeed so. You will remain on this ship as hostage."

"Hostage? That implies that you believe someone out there values me enough to accede to your demands to protect me. I can assure you; no such person is still alive in this time period."

"Not even Arlessa?"

"Arlessa?"

"The high priestess."

"I'm the high priestess. I should very much like to visit this Arlessa."

"I shall arrange it then. For now, I'll have quarters assigned to you, do not leave them until I send for you." With that he strode from the room and six armed guards entered, indicating she should follow them. Norlene smiled as she followed along. The Viceroy's quarters promised to be more comfortable than the cramped fighter ship. She might as well travel in style.

WHILE NORLENE RELAXED in comfort, Lessa was meeting with her new allies in her office. The chieftain of the Nara was there, as were the five former high priestesses. Their memories had returned, as had the memories of the lost years. Four just wanted to retire and enjoy their freedom; Marla wanted to roast the Viceroy alive.

They were trying to solidify their plans. The chieftain of the Nara was being evasive, however. He wanted to go along with Lessa's plan, but if it failed, both he and his clan would suffer beyond measure. "Lady, what you propose could upset the balance of power in this sector completely."

"Power is balanced in the region? Have I been out of touch for that long?"

"All right, Lessa, but if we fail, I'll be executed, and the clan will be exiled. This is the best we could hope for."

"Where's the thrill without the risk, Lortax?"

"It's been many years since I last heard you say that, Lessa. However, I have the people of the clan to consider."

"Yes, and I'm one of them." Lessa leaped to her feet, the rage dancing in her eyes as she fought for control. "At least I was one of them until the day your father sold me to the temple. I'm no fool, Lortax, I know why I was chosen to study at the temple. Even as a child that scum sucking son of a..."

Lessa stopped speaking and fought for control. Brenna reached out to gently squeeze her shoulder. Lessa gripped the hand on her shoulder for a moment, and then turned back to the chieftain. "The Viceroy wanted me even when I was a child. You know that's why I was sent to the temple."

"You're right, Lessa. It was your golden hair. I saw his face as he looked at you and it made my skin crawl. You were sent to the temple the next day." Suddenly Lortax burst out laughing. "He nearly died of apoplexy the day you vanished from the temple, one week before the wedding. I always knew you'd outsmart him, Lessa. All right, I'll back you here, but I get the office if we win."

"Agreed." Lessa's anger eased and she sank back into her chair. "Forgive my anger, Lortax. I have difficulty managing it where this man is concerned."

"Well, you'd better get a grip, Lessa. He'll see that weakness and take advantage. He'll taunt and bait you until you lose control then he'll strike."

"I know. Don't fear; I'll be ready. Marla, are you certain you want to take part in this mad scheme of ours? After what you've suffered, you have no need to take this on."

"I'll gladly serve you, Arlessa, for I can see Brenna was right. You're the greatest of us since the Black Witch. However, if you're set on this course, I'll gladly accept the task. After all, I do have experience."

"Yes you do," smiled Lessa. "Polina?"

"Marla was ever the most able high priestess before you came along. She and I once worked well together; I believe we can do so again. Marla, shall we begin to practice your part?"

"Yes, Polina, let's do. It has to be convincing."

"Very well then," smiled Lessa, "our plans are laid. Now we wait for our guest of honor to arrive."

"Do you think Gorda was successful?" Micha spoke aloud.

"Yes, Micha, he succeeded. I can feel her approach even now. They'll arrive on the morrow. Go now and set your traps." Micha nodded and left the room, followed closely by his crew. As they left, Lortax was looking carefully at Brenna.

"Something wrong, Chieftain?" He had been looking at her with a puzzled expression ever since she and Ena had returned with all the Viceroy's wives. "Forgive me, but that name sounds familiar. O'Loran. There is a standing reward, quite substantial, for any information leading to the return of a rich man's daughter. Apparently, he is some sort of big shot in the R.I.M. Company."

"Yes, my father is Vice-President of R.I.M., in charge of this sector, but he was expecting to get promoted soon."

"They believe you've been kidnapped and/or sold into slavery. His agents are combing the whole sector looking for you." Brenna shook her head. "I'll contact him as soon as this is all over. For now, my main concern is for Lessa."

"You're concerned for me? Why?"

"Forgive me, my love, but you seem a bit on edge since we've been re-united."

"It seems you've developed an edge of your own, my darling." Lessa reached out and stroked Brenna's cheek.

"I know. Lessa, when this is over, can we take a few years to get to know each other again, perhaps regain a bit of who we were?" Brenna reached for Lessa's fingers and squeezed them gently.

"You're right as usual, my dove. In the past two years I have been to places and done things I would rather forget, but they haunt me still. Yes, my love, I do need to exercise more control, especially now. Help me?"

"Any way I can, Lessa. What must I do?"

"Your touch is grounding, please stay close by my side."

"Of course I will, Lessa. What happened to you while you were gone?"

"A lot of seriously bad things, but I overcame them all. Norlene warned me it was too soon. She said I'd need a few years to gain full control. I believe she's right, but we don't have the luxury of that kind of time. Brenna, I never quite know what will trigger a rush of emotion, and anger drives a massive amount of power, but it's dark power. The cost of using it is too great, as I learned to my dismay. Stay with me, touch me if you sense me faltering."

"I will, my love, I will."

"Lessa, did you truly study with the Black Witch?"

"I did, Lortax, although study is not the best word. Trained is a much better word, for there was more doing than studying. In the end, I think I frightened her. Ah well, that was a time I do not wish to re-visit." Seeing the darkness in Lessa's eyes, Lortax took a step back.

"Forgiveness, Lessa, I will not ask again."

"Thank you, old friend. I don't mean to be so maudlin; it's the waiting that is driving me mad."

"Well then," smiled Brenna, "let's retire to chambers and I'll see if I can distract you."

"You will have no problem at all, Brenna, for I find you quite distracting."

As they were leaving, Micha and crew returned. "All is in readiness, Lessa. Nothing left to do now but wait for our guest. I truly hope he comes down to talk, as it'll be much more difficult if he just starts bombarding from space."

"He won't, Micha. This temple is the basis of his power. He won't dare destroy it. All the clans would rise up against him. No, he'll want to come down and put me in my place."

"Can you defeat him, Lessa?" Lortax asked softly.

"With ease, but he'll have a personal guard with him, at least six armed men. Micha must keep them out of the action."

"We'll take them out, don't worry, "Micha grinned. "All right, crew, get some rest. We have a big day tomorrow." They went to their separate chambers then, and prepared for sleep.

Micha was still pacing in their room when Edie put her arms around him from behind. "You must rest, Micha." "Sorry, Edie, my mind won't stop."

"You need a distraction." "I don't know. I'm pretty focused right now."

"Let me try, I'm sure I can think of something." She grinned then pulled him close and kissed him deeply. Micha wrapped his arms around her, his hands settling on her behind. Perhaps this is just what he needed, he thought, as Edie pressed herself against him. He angled Edie toward the bed then fell backwards, pulling her on top.

Edie giggled and asked, "What's this then?" as her hand closed on his manhood. "I think I've been distracted," he whispered before taking her mouth again. Later, as the young lovers lay spent in each other's arms, Edie cuddled closer. "Micha?"

"Mmm?" "Murtah always said you were the best farmer. Do you think we'll ever be able to go back to that?"

"As soon as Lessa's finished here, I believe that will be our fate. Nova will need farmers, and I'm tired of the wars. I'm certain you are as well."

"Yes, my love, I am. I'll be happy to get back to the land again." " As will I, pretty lady, as will I."

THE VICEROY WAS PACING and fuming. Curse that damned woman, why did she always make him come to her, and why did she always keep him waiting? She was infuriating! And yet there was something about her: she could certainly wield power. Perhaps she truly was the Black Witch. If so, she would make a powerful ally.

She didn't seem opposed to him, but neither would she commit her support. If driving him to madness was her goal, she was succeeding.

At last he heard the soft tap of her boots in the hallway. "Good morning, Viceroy. Have I kept you waiting long?"

"Indeed you have, Norlene."

"Well, you don't seem any worse for the wear. Are we there yet?"

"We will arrive at Borealis Prime within the hour."

"I should have thought you would be more excited than worried."

"Arlessa has slipped through my fingers far too many times for me to get excited. I'll celebrate when I have her in my hands."

"If she is as powerful as you say, perhaps those hands should be gentle."

"Are you suggesting I arrive and pretend like the past fifteen years have never happened?"

"What were you planning to do, attack Borealis Prime without provocation? I'm certain the clans would love that."

"They might rise up, and they might not. No matter if they do, I can defeat them."

"At what cost? History often speaks of men who fight too many battles on too many fronts at the same time. They are rarely victorious."

He sighed deeply and collapsed into a chair. She gracefully sat facing him. "You have the right of it, Norlene. Even if I defeat both Arlessa and the clans, my resources would be severely depleted. The war lords would band together and attack. With every faction in the sector weakened the companies would surely return. I know they're just waiting for us to destroy ourselves. "Very well then, I'll begin with a show of force to get their attention. Then I'll attack with guile and diplomacy. If that fails then I will destroy them all and start over. So, I ask you again, will you stand at my side?"

She thought for a moment and he sighed. She was going to evade him again. Norlene surprised him. "When you land and enter the temple, I'll walk by your side, Viceroy."

"Seriously? You will stand beside me in this?"

"I'm a woman out of time, sir. I need to make alliances, create a place for myself here."

"Excellent! Let us drink a toast to a successful day and a united sector. It's a bit early for spirits, but the water is excellent."

"To a successful day," she smiled as she raised her glass to touch his.

"To a successful day," he replied as their glasses clinked together. As they drank, the coms crackled and a voice announced their arrival. "Well, we seem to have arrived, are you ready?"

"No," he replied easily, "let them sweat a bit first."

POLINA HURRIED INTO Lessa's chambers. "Lady, the Viceroy has arrived with his armada."

"All right, here we go at last. Arouse my guardians and tell them to prepare."

"They're awaiting in your office now, Lady."

"Did I not tell you Micha would be well ahead of us, Brenna?"

"You did," she yawned as she sat up and ran her fingers through her hair.

"He and Edie are well matched then, for she's an early riser as well."

"I believe it is a result of growing up on a farm. Come, let us prepare ourselves for guests. Polina, please ask the Viceroy to wait in my outer office."

"He hasn't yet landed, Lady. The armada is in orbit, but no ship has requested landing instructions."

"Indeed. That's thoughtful of the man, allowing us time for a proper breakfast before begging an audience. Very well then, have food brought to the office. If he wishes to play the waiting game, we'll play."

As she and Brenna reached the office there was mad confusion inside. Micha and his crew were trying to hit each other, and failing.

The speed of their movements could not be followed, they were all a blur. "So kiddies, enjoying your enhancements?"

"Just practicing, Lessa," puffed Micha as they all stopped, breathing deeply. "Lady, don't mistake me for ungrateful, but may I ask why you enhanced us so?"

"Murtah, I've dragged you all into something greater than yourselves. You've all put your lives and the lives of your loved ones at great risk. Should this go badly, I've given you all I have to give, the power to help you survive."

"How long with these enhancements last, Lady?"

"As long as you and your line last, Ena. This will pass through the generations. Should you survive to bear more children, you must teach them to use their gifts wisely."

"Lessa, forgive me, but are you saying we're the beginnings of a super race?"

"Yes, Micha, I am. If we're successful here this day, you and your crew will become the guardians of Nova, a race of exceptional warriors devoted to the protection of Nova Prime. Novans will never be enslaved again."

Micha was quiet for a moment, thoughtful. At last he met her eyes and spoke. "I accept this responsibility. Crew?"

"Accepted," they all agreed. They were subdued as they reflected on the magnitude of what they had been chosen to do. They ate quietly when the food arrived, absorbed in their own thoughts. The last of the food disappeared as Polina returned. "The Viceroy's spokesman has requested permission to land and announced the Viceroy seeks an audience with the High Priestess."

"So it begins. Have the Viceroy brought to the audience chamber. Micha, are you ready?"

"Ready, Lessa. All right, crew, positions." They filed out of the room and vanished into the corridors.

"Lady, you enhanced them? Arlessa, do you know what you've done?"

"Yes, Polina, I've made certain Nova will never be enslaved again. They'll be the new Novans, and they will live free, even if I don't survive."

Brenna didn't like the sound of this and turned to Lessa, her face filled with concern. "Don't fret, my beloved, I can deal with the Viceroy. It's his armada that concerns me. If they accept my orders then all will be well, but if they try to rescue or avenge the Viceroy, we might well be bombarded from space. Our fate under such circumstances would be uncertain at best. Will you not relent and let me send you to safety?"

"I've been in war zones before, Lessa. I won't leave your side."

"All right, my darling, together it is. Let's go now to the Hall of Audience. I believe we're expecting company."

———————⎯◉⎯———————

AS THE VICEROY'S PERSONAL craft left his warship to go down to the planet, Gorda suddenly dropped beneath it, keeping the Viceroy's ship as a shield. "What the nine hells of Porapix is that damned fool pilot of yours doing? He'll get us all killed."

"Relax," Norlene chuckled.

"My ship goes where I go. He's just making sure one of your gunships doesn't decide to blow him out of the sky. Gorda will escort us to the ground."

"You have more faith in his abilities than I do. Where did you get an Arcalian fighter ship? That looks like one of the King's own guards."

"It is. Now stop asking questions I will not answer and think about how you are going to approach this. We are almost on the ground."

"I have a plan, don't worry. By the end of this day you will be High Priestess again and I'll have a new bride, one I have desired for many years." There was a gentle bump as the ship landed.

They descended to the ground; Gorda was standing by his fighter not far away. He smiled as Norlene winked at him. A moment later the Viceroy got his first setback. A woman came out to greet them; it wasn't the woman he expected.

"You! What are you doing in the robes of Regent?"

"In the name of Arlessa, High Priestess, I greet you, Viceroy. To answer your question, I am now the Regent."

"Where is Salian?"

"She attacked the High Priestess. She now languishes in the prison below the temple. If you will follow me please, I'll escort you to the Hall of Audience."

"I'd prefer to meet with the High Priestess in the privacy of her offices."

"She would not. I've been instructed to take you to the Hall of Audience. That's where the High Priestess is now, and she will receive you there or not at all. These are her instructions. Leave your armed guards here."

She turned and walked away. The Viceroy followed, and at his signal, so did his guards. Norlene walked at his side. As they headed down the long corridor, Norlene smiled. Only she had been aware that two of the guards had disappeared from the back of the group. A few dozen steps later, there were no more armed guards left with them.

They arrived at the Hall of Audience and were instructed to wait at the entryway. The High Priestess was hearing another petition. The Viceroy got his second shock then. The petitioner was one of his wives, Marla. How had she gotten free of the inhibitor and how had she managed to get here? Rage welled up within him as he heard Arlessa speak.

"I deem your petition for divorcement from your mate on the grounds of cruelty to be valid, Marla. I pronounce you a free woman and declare you entitled to one fourth the man's wealth. Is this satisfactory to you?"

"Thank you, Lady Arlessa, it's more than fair."

"You will have a bloody hard time collecting that, Marla. How did you get here?" the Viceroy demanded.

"In a spaceship, actually," she replied, a snarl on her lips. As he strode toward her, a fireball appeared in her hand. "Go ahead, strike me again. It won't be so easy now."

"Hold," said Lessa as she rose to her feet. "Marla." Marla closed her hand and the fireball vanished. "Now, who is this man?"

"You know damned well who I am, Arlessa. I'm the Viceroy."

"Actually, you are not, for I've declared the post open this very day. I have another, more able man in mind for the job. Marla, who is this person?"

"This is my former mate, Lady Arlessa," smiled Marla. "I see. Since you are here at these proceedings, can I assume you wish to make a counter petition?"

"What?? No. Wait! Yes."

"Which is it?"

"Yes!"

"I will hear you," replied Lessa as she sat back in her high seat. Marla was almost giggling. Arlessa's strategy of putting him on the defensive was clearly working well. The Viceroy was now very far away from the conversation he had planned to have with the High Priestess. "You may speak."

"I'm here to claim you, Arlessa, as is the custom."

"You will speak to the petition before me or not at all. Do you, or do you not wish to oppose this woman's claim of cruelty?"

"Yes," he snarled, fighting to keep his composure.

"I deny these allegations and desire to return her to her rightful place in my home."

"Marla, you may speak to the charge you bring."

"Thank you, Lady Arlessa. As you know, I was High Priestess, and after three years in office, I agreed to the sacrifice. I was joined to this man and removed to his home. There I was fitted with an inhibitor, an instrument that robbed me of my senses and made me completely compliant to all his wishes."

"You were unwilling?"

"I accepted the inhibitor as is the tradition, Lady, but his desires are violent, and I would never have submitted to him had there been no inhibitor."

"So, the inhibitor was used, not only to curtail your use of power, but to subject you to humiliation and cruelty as well?"

"Indeed so, Lady."

"Well then, how do you respond, sir?"

"That is all a pack of lies. My men will attest to it."

"Are these men with you to testify?"

"They are. Come forward." There was a snicker through the assembled priestesses. He spun around and only then realized his men were gone.

"Well," demanded Lessa as he spun back to face her.

"They've disappeared. What have you done with them?"

"I've done nothing with your men. Do you deny you used an inhibitor on this woman?"

"No I don't deny it. Of course I used the inhibitor. What man in his right mind wouldn't?"

"Then, by your own admission I find you guilty of cruelty. My judgment stands. Next petition, please."

"Now wait just a damned minute here," sputtered the Viceroy. "I'm not finished here."

"Yes you are," thought Brenna with amusement, but she said nothing.

"What is it?"

"Forget this foolishness, Arlessa. I've come to claim you. Stop all this posturing and submit to the inhibitor. You're mine and you can no longer escape that fact."

"I am already claimed and joined," she replied coldly as she faced him. He actually shrank back from the rage dancing in her eyes. "My mate is Brenna O'Loran, a high born daughter of the R.I.M. Company. Your claim is denied."

That was another shock. The last thing he had expected was to find her allied with the very company that had destroyed her home world. "Now, if there are no further petitions, I will move on to an appointment. Let the chieftain of Nara Clan step forward." Lortax stepped forward. He was braced for the worst, but determined, none the less.

"Lortax, Chieftain of Nara Clan, loyal servant of the Temple, the position of Viceroy is now open since the previous man has admitted his guilt and plans to commit treason. Yesterday you assured me of your willingness to ascend to this position. Will you now accept the post and the responsibilities inherent therein?"

"I will, Lady Arlessa."

"Now just a damned minute here..."

"Then I pronounce you, Lortax, Viceroy of the Ninth Sector. You will now assume your duties and place this man in custody. Put an inhibitor on him and deliver him to the dungeons."

"I'd like to see you try..." "You will remove your chain of office and pass it to Lortax, then submit yourself to the inhibitor."

"Enough of this foolishness," roared the Viceroy as he flung out his arms. A burst of power sent Marla crashing into the wall where she sank, groaning, to the floor. Lessa was hurled back several feet and driven to her knees. "Norlene, take care of that one while I deal with Arlessa. You will stay right there while I put the inhibitor on you. I've had enough of this madness. This night you will be on my ship behaving as my wife. Norlene!"

"I have everything under control here," replied the Black Witch as she bent over the fallen Marla. She winked mischievously and held out her hands. Marla grasped those hands tentatively and felt a surge of power course through her. She rose to her feet stronger than she had ever been. Brenna's heart was in her mouth and she started forward. She was suddenly frozen still, unable to move or utter a sound. After a moment's struggle she felt the eyes of the Black Witch on her. Upon meeting that gaze she was startled to see the merriment in those eyes. The witch winked then released her.

Brenna backed away again. As Brenna backed away, the Viceroy was bellowing for an inhibitor to be brought forward. "Bring it now, or I'll simply kill the witch." He was holding Lessa down with an enormous flow of power. She was strong and it was taxing his ability to hold her. "Where is that damned inhibitor?"

"No one here will obey or aid you, Traitor," said Lessa as she stood back on her feet. He redoubled his effort, but couldn't force her down. "Norlene." The Viceroy was struggling against Arlessa's flow of power.

"Yes?" "Your assistance is needed here."

"Is it? Arlessa seems to be doing fine without me. Do you need assistance, Lessa?"

"Not at this time, my mentor. I believe I have things well in hand." His eyes bulged and the veins on his forehead stood out with the effort expended, but Lessa brushed his hold aside and stepped toward him. She reached out and slowly closed her hand in the air. His arms were forced to his sides and he couldn't move.

"Viceroy Lortax, bring that inhibitor here and place it on this traitor."

"Yes Lady, as you command." Lessa held the struggling man still until the inhibitor was implanted at the base of his skull and adjusted. He whimpered twice then relaxed, all the tension leaving his body as his eyes went blank. Lessa waved her hand and her high seat leaped from where it had fallen and resumed its accustomed place.

"Now then, bring him here so we can get some information from this fellow," she said as she sat gracefully and gestured that the former Viceroy be brought before her. Lortax removed the chain of office and placed it around his own neck, then guided the man to a place in front of Lessa. As he was placed before her, Lessa leaned closer and spoke directly to him.

"You will answer all my questions truthfully."

"Yes."

Lessa sighed then gazed at him for a long moment. He did not move at all. "Tell me," she said at last, "why did you pursue me for so long?"

"Wanted you."

"What made me so special?"

"Beautiful child with golden hair. Very rare."

"Indeed. Was it you who had me sent to the temple?"

"Yes."

"Why?"

"It was the only way. They refused to sell you to me."

"Who refused to sell me."

"Your parents."

"Did you send them back to Nova Prime?"

"Yes, it was barely in time."

"In time for what?"

"The cleansing."

"The cleansing? Do you mean the massacre of everyone on the planet?"

"Yes."

"You knew this would happen?"

"Yes." The rage was starting to overpower Lessa and she began to tremble with the effort to hold herself in check. "Arlessa." Norlene's voice cut like a knife and Lessa's eyes snapped up to lock with hers. For a moment it looked as though she would attack, but Brenna lightly placed a hand on her shoulder. Lessa broke eye contact with Norlene and looked at the small dark hand on her arm. She sighed deeply and kissed those fingers before turning back.

"I've heard enough, take him away."

"Wait, there's more, much more."

"Brenna?"

"I know all too well how these plots work. Allow me to question him; he has more to tell us yet."

"As you wish. You will answer this woman's questions truthfully."

"Yes."

Brenna gave him a hard look before she spoke. "Did you have any involvement with the massacre on Nova Prime?"

"Yes."

"What was it?"

"It was my idea. I provided the poison gasses."

"Explain."

"Nova was rebelling. The company didn't have the resources to control the sector. I went to a company man with a plan. We would poison Nova Prime. All others would rise up, the company would withdraw, and I would keep the factions warring amongst themselves. I would have great wealth and power and the company would not waste resources."

"The man who liked your plan, what was his name?"

"O'Loran."

"Of all the..."

"There's more, Lessa. Tell me, do you have contacts here in the temple?"

"Yes."

Brenna held up a small recording device. "Name them." He did so, then she passed the recorder to Lessa who passed it to Polina. There would be five more people in deep trouble before this day was finished. "Do you still have contact with the company?"

"Yes."

"Why?"

"They send money and weapons for the wars."

"Why do they want the wars?"

"To keep the factions from uniting against them when they return. The wars keep them weak."

There was a snarl from Lortax at this. "Who is your company contact?"

"My secretary, he's my controller. He reports to C.E.O. O'Loran and brings me instructions."

Brenna turned away, tears in her eyes. As a child she had looked up to her father, but now he sickened her. "I'm done, Lessa. I think that's about all we'll get out of him."

"Take him away, Lortax. Micha!"

"Right here, Lessa."

"Have you any prisoners?"

"There are six fellows here who worked for the Viceroy. I'm sure they could be convinced to work for the new guy."

"Bring them forward." Micha waved his hand and the crew brought the six men to her. "You are loyal to the Viceroy?"

"We're soldiers, Lady. We serve the office, not the man."

"So you have no objection to serving the new Viceroy?"

"None Lady."

She gazed into his eyes for a long moment then sat back. "You are accepted. This man is now the Viceroy. Your tasks will be set by him."

"Understood Lady."

"They're all yours, Lortax."

"Thank you, High Priestess. I should now like to go up and inspect the armada. May I borrow your personal guards, just in case there are a few dissenters in the ranks?"

Lessa grinned at that. "Micha, take the crew and go with the Viceroy. Remain until you're fairly certain all is well."

"Aye Lady. All right crew, let's go up and see this armada first hand."

Lessa waited until they had left the hall before she spoke again. "Now then, good people, we have one last piece of business to attend to. In the near future I and my mentor, Norlene, will remove ourselves to Nova Prime where we will construct a small satellite temple for the use of Novans. However, we will not leave this temple without her High Priestess. Marla, come forward."

With a look of shock on her face, Marla stepped forward. "Lady?"

"Marla, will you accept the mantle of high priestess, to take this high seat on the day I leave for Nova Prime?"

"Arlessa, are you serious?"

"I am. It was often whispered that you were the best in generations. You're young still; you have plenty of good years left and the Temple needs a high priestess."

"Will you not stay?"

"My focus is to re-build Nova Prime, Marla. This should be your sector once again. You can trust Lortax to back you, and together I think you can bring peace to the region. Will you take this on?"

"Yes, if that is your wish. May I ask for your help if things get out of hand?"

"Of course, all temples respond to the call of the high priestess. Nova Prime's will be no different."

"In that case I will do my utmost to bring honor and dignity to the office and peace to the sector."

"Then it's decided. Let us now retire to my office for a meal and a rest. It's been a taxing morning."

"Should we not remain on our guard, just in case the armada is less than welcoming to the new Viceroy?" Marla queried.

"Not to worry, Marla," laughed Norlene. "Lessa's pet savages will keep the armada under control. Let's go eat, I'm hungry." They returned to Lessa's office where they found Brenna, curled up in a chair by the fireplace, tears running freely down her cheeks. She was in Lessa's arms in an instant.

"Brenna, oh my Brenna..."

"Lessa, how can you stand to touch me, knowing what my father has done, and what he continues to do?"

"How could I not touch you when you set my soul ablaze? Brenna, my heart, you're not your father, nor do you control his actions." Lessa continued to hold her until the emotion subsided. Marla brought some fruit and, though reluctantly at first, Brenna began to nibble on it.

Marla returned to her seat and sat gazing at Norlene. "You have a question, High Priestess?"

"Marla, please. Call me Marla. Are you truly the Black Witch, the most powerful and feared high priestess in a hundred generations?"

"I am she, or I was until Arlessa came along. I've been seriously outclassed."

"Stop it, Norlene. Don't listen to her, Marla. She's all laughter and teasing until something angers her. Never make her angry, terrible things happen, too terrible to speak of."

"You're a fine one to talk, Lessa. Don't forget, I've seen what you're capable of when you lose your temper. I hope never to see that again."

"You will not, for my Brenna won't let me lose control. She'll keep me grounded until I master the control I need."

"Control?" It was Brenna who had spoken. Norlene sighed, and then spoke when Lessa didn't.

"Arlessa needs to learn full control of her emotions, Brenna. Lessa's learned in two years what it took me twenty to master. Her new grasp of power is a bit, shall we say, undisciplined as yet? She'll be just fine in a few years or so."

"A few years? Lessa?"

"I had to get back to you, my Brenna. There was no time without a shift, and by then the age difference between us could have become an issue."

Brenna put her arms around Lessa and laid her head on the taller woman's shoulder. "It wouldn't, but I'm glad you did not wait longer, my love. We'll deal with your temper together."

Lessa kissed her hair as she felt the small giggle at her shoulder. "It's bad luck to tease a cranky witch." She smiled and hugged her lover tightly.

Back to Nova

The Viceroy's shuttle rose gracefully from the launch pad, escorted by two Arcalian fighters bearing the forbidden colors of Nova Prime. No one in the entire fleet fired a shot for fear of hitting the shuttle. Everyone relaxed as the coms came to life and one of the Viceroy's personal guards came on screen.

"Prepare for the Viceroy's return and ship inspection."

"Ship inspection? What ship inspection?"

"The Viceroy wishes to inspect the entire fleet, beginning with the Dragon's Wing. Have his ship ready and guest quarters prepared."

He broke the connection and the captain sighed. "He must have the witch and wants to show her off," he muttered. "Attention all hands, prepare for ship inspection, full burn."

He was still muttering as he and his senior officers plus an honor guard hurried to the docking port for an official greeting. They all got a shock as a stranger wearing the chain of office of the Viceroy stepped through the door, followed by the Viceroy's personal guard and five heavily armed mercenaries.

"I demand to know what is going on here," said the captain as he stepped up to the stranger.

"And I will tell you," replied Lortax. "I'm the newly appointed Viceroy. I'm Lortax of Nara, and I'm now in command here. The former Viceroy is in prison beneath the temple, an inhibitor clamped to his head. Unless you wish to join him there, this will be the last time you demand anything from me, understood?"

The captain gulped as he tried to absorb this information. He considered putting up a fight, but his people weren't armed and these mercs looked dangerous.

Suddenly one of the mercs moved. Before anyone could register that he had indeed moved, he was standing beside the captain with a blaster pointed at his head. "The Viceroy is waiting for your reply."

The captain swallowed hard then choked out a single word. "Understood."

Lortax looked the man in the eye for a moment then stepped past him to the officers. "Who is First Man here?"

"I am, sir. First Officer Koda, at your service sir."

"Tell me Koda, do you serve the office or the man?"

"Sir, I serve the office. May I confirm your story?"

"You may. Do you wish to contact the temple?"

"Unnecessary, Sir. I trust these men." He turned to the Viceroy's personal guard. "Speak."

"The former Viceroy attacked and was defeated then put in prison by the High Priestess Arlessa. She has appointed this man to the post. We serve the office, not the man."

He turned back to Lortax, a slight smile on his face. "I serve both the office and the man, sir, in that order."

Lortax laughed heartily. "All right, I promote you to Captain. Captain Koda, get that demanding fool off your ship, then take me to the bridge. I wish to address the Armada."

"Sir, if I may, perhaps we should confer for a moment before you address the fleet."

Lortax nodded. "All right, Captain Koda. Let's do exactly that. Please bring the two Arcalian fighter ships aboard and have the pilots join us."

Koda barked a few orders then led them to a large room, deep within the huge ship. "This is the ship's meeting room. The Former Viceroy often met with the ship's officers or guests here."

"Very comfortable," mused Micha.

"Too comfortable for my taste," muttered Lortax. "All right, Captain, speak your piece."

"Viceroy, there are factions within the fleet who will remain loyal to your predecessor, that or attempt to wrest control from you."

"Tell me all of it."

"There are company spies on every ship. The companies will be aware of your every move. I expect one or more to contact you soon. If you refuse to co-operate with them, they'll either attempt to have the former Viceroy reinstated, you assassinated, or they could come to the sector in force and do it themselves."

"So, the former captain was a company man?"

"Completely."

"And you?"

"I'm Novan by birth."

"All right, Captain. Ena?"

"He speaks truly." Ena had been right at Lortax's side since they entered the ship. He valued her talent and wanted no surprises.

"Very good. Captain, do you know who the spies are on your ship?"

"There were two. You demoted the first; I'll deal with the other."

"As you wish. Tell me, what are we facing here?"

"At worst, full scale rebellion, at best, the only battle will be political. I hope you're good at that."

"So do I."

Suddenly the claxon sounded, and battle stations were called. Lortax and his retinue followed the captain to the bridge.

"Report!" barked the captain as he arrived amid the scene of organized chaos.

"Incoming fleet sir."

"What colors?"

"Borealis and Nova sir."

"Stand down battle stations. Those are my people come to join the fleet." All eyes turned to Lortax. "I'm the newly appointed Viceroy. This man, as you probably already know is your new captain. Those are my ships. Please contact the Colton's Captain, Borad."

"Sir!" The coms operator was busy for a moment, and then a tall bearded man came on screen. "This is Captain Borad of the Colton. Who Commands this fleet?"

"I do, Captain Borad," said Lortax as he stepped before the vid screen. "I'm Viceroy Lortax, recently appointed to the post by the high priestess of the temple."

"I see that all went well, my chieftain," chuckled the captain. "Permission to join the fleet?"

"Granted. This man is Captain Koda; he commands the fleet. I leave you to it gentlemen."

As he turned away, Koda spoke softly. "Viceroy?"

"You know this fleet and her people, Captain. I don't want any battles if they can be avoided, but I won't compromise. The fleet is yours, take command."

"Aye Sir."

In less than three hours, Koda had managed to get full control of all the Viceroy's forces. The threat of rebellion was greatly diminished by the presence of the Nara clan in full force. Ekta clan had quickly thrown in with Nara and the fleet fell into line. Most of the people were shocked at having a new Viceroy, but after a moment to reflect, had no problem serving under him.

"You seem relieved, Koda."

"I am. I know many of the other captains and am happy that we don't have to kill each other. The arrival of clan forces was most helpful. What are your orders now?"

"Send them all home for now, Captain. I'm certain the high priestess will have lots for us all to do in the days to come, so keep them on alert, but let them go home. No one dies today."

"Then it's a good day, Viceroy. It shall be as you command. Shall I keep the clan forces here?"

"No, let them go. We will remain for we have some passengers to deliver to Nova Prime very soon."

"Nova Prime? Sir?"

"The air is clear there now, Captain. There are folk returning there to rebuild. Spread the word through the fleet that Novans may return home now if they wish."

"I will be more than happy to, Viceroy. That's good news indeed."

<hr />

THE NEXT MORNING SAW the Viceroy's shuttle rising from the temple once again. This time it carried Lessa, Brenna, Marla, and Norlene. Once aboard, they all gathered in the Viceroy's meeting room. "All right folks, we're gathered for a while to lay our plans."

"We've succeeded, Lessa," smiled Lortax. "Don't you want to enjoy the victory for a while before you start scheming again?"

"There's no time, Lortax, and well you know it. Your task is to solidify your position and unite the factions. With Marla's help you should be able to bring them all into line."

"Peace in the sector. Lessa, isn't that shooting for the stars?" Lortax asked.

"You know as well as I do that if things continue the way they have been, the companies will be able to walk back in and enslave the lot of us. We must be able to show a united front."

"I know you're right. It's just the magnitude of the task that gives me the shivers."

"We can do it, Lortax," smiled Marla. "I want to be involved as much as possible in all the negotiations. I was once very good at that sort of thing, before..."

"Lady Marla, I'll be more than thrilled to let you take the lead on this. I'm no politician. You be the brains, and I'll provide the brawn. Together we shall succeed."

"Now you're talking sense, Viceroy. It'll be good to use my brain after all these years of growing mold. Arlessa, can we call on you if we need help?"

"Of course you can. Nova Temple will always answer the call of the High Priestess."

"What of your mercenaries, Lessa. They're a seriously effective crew; I'd like to keep them."

"Forgive me, Viceroy," Micha chimed in, "but I serve Lady Arlessa only. Actually, I think the whole crew is ready to go farming." At this point a man came in and whispered to the captain.

"What? Quickly, spit it out so all can hear."

"Aye, Sir. A message has come on a secure channel from the Viceroy, I mean former Viceroy. He and the Lady Salian have escaped and have acquired a ship. They are on their way to Borealis Two where he'll be able to defend himself against all attacks. We're commanded to take the fleet and meet him there."

"Perhaps we should do just that," grinned Lortax.

"No, I think Arlessa wants to do this herself," smiled Marla. "I think we should be about our assigned tasks. Lessa and her crew will deal with the escaped prisoner."

"If that is your wish, Lady Marla," grinned Lessa, "then we shall do our best to retrieve the prisoners. Come crew, to the fighters." Lortax chuckled as he overheard Zartah on the way out. "See, Murtah, like I said, there's always something exciting to do with this crew."

THE TWO ARCALIAN FIGHTERS swept into Borealis Two's atmosphere and dropped low as they skimmed the surface below detection sensors. "All right, Micha, get us in there and I'll deal with my old enemy. Getting us there and keeping the distractions away is your job."

"I suppose I get to subdue the former regent while you have all the fun."

"Yes, Norlene, but you will also have to protect Brenna."

"I'm not a child, Lessa. I'm a full member of Micha's crew, and I'll do my part as the boss directs. I'll be fine."

"Am I not allowed to worry about you at all?" Lessa cupped Brenna's cheek before kissing it lightly.

Brenna took Lessa's hand in hers and squeezed it hard. "No, you need to focus. You know he'll try to play your emotions against you. If you lose your temper and drop your guard..."

"I know, dear Brenna, I know."

"Miss O'Loran."

"Yes Micha?"

"Your assignment is to guard the Lady Arlessa and keep her out of trouble."

"Yes boss," grinned Brenna. "I hear and obey."

"Gorda, set us down a day's march out from the house. He'll have all sorts of enchantments guarding the place, and I want plenty of time for the Ladies in Black to find and disable them."

"Aye boss, a day's march out it is."

The two ships swept over the landscape for half a continent, then gracefully touched down in a small valley. Keira was first on the ground, making a fast sweep of the area. Murtah and Zartah followed then all the others came out and stretched out the kinks.

"All right people, here we go. I'll take point with Edie and Keira in second. Murtah, Ena, and Zartah, you've got our rear. Gorda, you're assigned to Lady Norlene as personal guard."

"Aye boss. I'll try to keep her out of trouble."

"Careful, Gorda, it's dangerous to tease a Black Witch. I might turn you into a toad," threatened Norlene, shaking her finger at him even as she smiled.

"Yes, Ma'am, I don't know what came over me."

"Let's go people!" Micha headed out, with Edie and Keira a few paces behind him. Everyone else followed. They walked for hours, following Micha who was ever watchful. From time to time he'd consult his positioning device then slightly alter course.

They stopped for rest twice then made camp under the trees near a stream. Micha disappeared for a while then returned. "This won't be easy, Lessa."

"Tell us."

"I found the palace. It's surrounded by walls, gun placements, and is guarded by dozens of armed men. Fourteen fighter ships are parked outside the walls as are ten troop transports."

"So, we go in after dark boss?" asked Zartah.

"After dark tomorrow. Tonight and tomorrow is for rest and recon."

"You want a couple of us to go back for the ships and create a diversion boss?" asked Gorda.

"No, I don't think we need to do that. After all, we have the Black Witch of legend here with us, I'm sure she can create a diversion for us. Lady Norlene?"

"Oh, that shouldn't be a problem, Micha. Gorda and I will create a diversion for you."

"Me?"

"Yes, Gorda. I'll be getting into all sorts of mischief; I'll need you to make sure they don't get me. After all, I am nine generations old you know, I'm not as spry as I once was."

Zartah elbowed Gorda in the ribs, "There's always something exciting to do on this crew."

As the sun began to set the next day, the entire crew checked their weapons and set out for the palace. It was completely dark when they arrived at the perimeter of the lighted security area outside the walls.

Staying just out of the light, Norlene and Gorda moved to the left and headed for the main gate. Lessa and the crew went right looking for another way in. Norlene seemed a bit out of focus as they neared the main gate. "Lady, are you well?"

"Fine, Gorda. Come closer to me, touch my hand, and look at the air before the gates." He did so and was startled to see a greenish glow surrounding the entire mansion, but thicker at the gate. "It's a magical barrier. If you touch it you get fried."

"Good to know," he whispered. "What do we do?"

"Tear it down. We're the diversion aren't we?"

"Yes Ma'am; that we are. What do I do?"

"Once I start those thugs will come boiling out of there, guns a blazing. You have to keep them off me for a few moments, and then we'll surrender."

"Surrender?"

"Of course. All eyes will be on us and the commotion. By the time our friend realizes who he's captured, Lessa and the crew will be inside. The fur will fly then. We'll break loose and take down the former regent. That's our job. You ready?"

Gorda checked his weapons, then stretched out on the ground. He laid three beside him, released the safeties then nodded. He was as ready as he could be. He focused his attention on the gate. Norlene stood up and strode toward the gate, keeping well out of his line of fire. She began to chant in a strong voice, and he felt the air crackle around him.

The magic barrier became visible then began to waver as she continued chanting even stronger. Suddenly, with a sound like thunder, the barrier collapsed and vanished. Armed men came pouring out of the gate, but Gorda laid down heavy fire, holding them back. When down to his last weapon he strode toward Norlene, firing steadily. He was at her side as the weapon emptied its last round. A moment later armed men came pouring out of the gate. They were instantly surrounded.

"Get on the ground, now!" bellowed one man as he shoved a weapon in Gorda's face. As he turned to comply, the man grabbed

Norlene to throw her down. "I said get on the ground now." The man's face exploded under Gorda's fist.

The others were stunned at his speed and strength as Gorda had the soldier's weapon, dismantled it, and threw it on the ground. "Don't touch the lady."

Norlene looked at him for a moment then smiled. "I could have handled that, but then you'd just get lazy and dependent."

"And we wouldn't want that to happen, now would we," he grinned.

"That's enough! Get inside, both of you. One false move and we'll open fire."

"Understood," Norlene replied nodding. They were marched through the gate and toward the main house.

LESSA HELD UP HER CLOSED fist and everyone froze in place. Soon they heard the rattle of gunfire and Lessa gave them the signal to go. Norlene had the barrier down. They reached the wall surrounding the mansion; Micha locked his fingers and launched Murtah to the top. One by one they leaped and were hauled up and over by Murtah.

Once inside, Lessa led them on a zigzag course through the magical traps until they reached the house. A moment at the lock and Keira had the door open. They were all inside.

The crew split up and began their search. Each servant or slave they found was quickly silenced, gagged, and bound. The first floor was cleared before they heard the mad screaming from above.

"You've got the Black Witch? You bloody fools! She's a diversion. How else could you have caught her? Get in here now and guard the stairwell. Shoot the witch."

Micha lunged toward the door, but Lessa caught his arm. "Trust Norlene. They won't harm her." Weapons fire could be heard from outside, then the terrified screams of men. Micha nodded then turned his attention to the staircase. Armed men were pouring down.

Micha darted into view then vanished through a door. Several men gave chase. A dozen or more men poured through that doorway then met their fate at the hands of the crew. There were a few grunts, screams, and a lot of crashing. The crew emerged wearing a few bruises, cuts and scrapes, but were all still in fine fighting shape.

The few men who had remained on the stairs were frozen stiff, unable to move, held fast in Lessa's magical grip. The main door opened and Norlene stepped inside, followed by Gorda.

The crew was busy putting the captives on the stairs in restraints. Suddenly a blast of energy sent everyone tumbling down the stairs. "This is all very amusing, Arlessa," snarled the former Viceroy, "but the game is over. I'm in my own lair now, and I'm more than ready for you.

"I knew you would come, you see. Last time we dueled on your turf, but without the energy of the temple and all the priestesses to call upon, things will be different here. Salian, use your enhanced powers to subdue that traitorous Black Witch."

A blast of power struck Norlene and sent her crashing into the wall. Gorda leaped at the stairs, but was battered down instantly. Norlene floated easily to the floor and raised him up, then dusted off his collar. "Perhaps I'll let you handle this one," Gorda groaned.

"That's my good lad. I won't be but a moment." She turned and took another blast of energy, but brushed it aside. Thrusting out her hand, Norlene sent Salian crashing back into the wall, her body crushed to a pulp, lifeless. "Annoying little shit," she muttered, "who the hell did she think she was playing with anyway?"

The former Viceroy's eyes opened wide in surprise at that. Dear gods, the power that woman could wield. He turned and fled down the hallway. Lessa gave chase with Brenna close behind. As the rest of the crew surged forward Norlene stopped them. "Easy does it, warriors, best not to get in the way of a magical duel."

"What about Miss O'Loran?"

"She still has a part to play here, Micha. Don't worry, Lessa will protect her."

"Can he win, Lady?"

"Not on his best day with ten more to help him, Micha. Stop being such a worrier. I know, I know, protector of the high priestess and all that, but she can handle this one."

"All right, if you say so, but I don't like it."

"It's alright boss," Gorda offered. "Sometimes you just have to let a witch fight her own battle." Norlene chuckled and patted Gorda's shoulder. Since all they could do was wait, Edie began bandaging up their injuries. Upstairs they could hear the cracking of beams and walls as the battle raged.

Lessa ran down the hall with Brenna close behind her. They stopped and then turned to the left, following a chanting voice. Two rooms down they found him standing inside a circle of salt. He was chanting in some foul language and a mist was beginning to take on a hideous shape.

Lessa sent a bolt of energy at it, the demon howled in pain then vanished again. The former Viceroy turned and with a snarl on his face, sent a blast of energy at Lessa, pushing her back. Lessa righted herself and sent a blast in return that should have put him on his knees.

"Ha! I'm much stronger here, Arlessa, and within the circle, stronger still." He sent another blast at her and she was rocked back again.

"I've had about enough of your games," Lessa growled and hit him with another wave of energy. This time he staggered back. The next blast she sent drove him to his knees. Catching a movement out of the corner of his eye, the Viceroy looked to see that Brenna had kicked a hole in his circle. Realizing his increased vulnerability, he shot out his hand and Brenna was thrust towards him by a force she couldn't name. He had her by the throat in an instant.

"Back off, Arlessa, back off or I'll snap her neck." He struggled to his feet, still holding Brenna by the throat, keeping her between himself and the witch. Lessa backed off. "Get on your knees, witch." As Lessa sank to her knees, the Viceroy was startled to hear Brenna's choked voice.

"Look into my eyes."

"What??" For only an instant he met her eyes then felt the prick in his side. Glancing down he saw the syringe sticking out between his ribs. Wide eyed, he looked back at her then fell dead on the floor.

As his hand left her neck, Brenna rubbed the feeling back into her throat. She kicked the fallen body. "Two men have put their hands on my throat," she snarled. "Both have met the same fate." She kicked the body harder. "I'm Brenna Eileen O'Loran, and I'm a dispatcher. Touch me at your own peril." She kicked the body again then turned and stepped away, straight into Lessa's arms.

"Brenna..."

"Hush now, my beloved Lessa, I knew I might end up as a pawn in this game. I also knew that, if either he or Salian used me as a shield, you wouldn't fight nor defend yourself. I brought two charges with me, one for each if needed."

"Oh Brenna..."

"You once told me to learn survival skills, and I've done so. Lessa I..."

She got no further as Lessa kissed her gently. "I love this new Brenna," she whispered as their lips slowly parted, "just as I did the old one. I'm so very proud of the fierce and strong woman you've become, my darling. Let's leave this accursed place and go home."

"Home?"

"To Nova. We have a farm to help build." She put her arm around Brenna and stepped to the doorway.

"I'd love nothing more than to spend a few years on a farm again," smiled Brenna as they descended the stairs.

"Then we shall make it so. Come Brenna, our business here is complete. Let's go home to Nova and get a crop in the ground."

They found Norlene and the crew back on the ground floor. Edie had already patched up what few injuries they had incurred. Micha looked up as they descended the stairs. "He dead, Lessa?"

"He's dead," she replied. "He tried to use Brenna as a shield. She dispatched him swiftly."

"Remind me not to annoy your mate, Lessa," chuckled Norlene.

"So, are we all done here, Lessa?"

"Yes we are, Micha."

"All right. Zartah, see if you can find us a vehicle, I'm too tired to walk back to the ships. All this fighting has worn me out."

"Aye, Boss," chuckled Zartah as he slipped through the door.

"So what's our next move, Lessa?"

"We go home to Nova Prime, Micha," she smiled. "Norlene and I have a temple to build, and your crew has a farm to establish."

"Now there's an idea I can embrace," he smiled as they heard the rumble of a land transport outside. Zartah sounded the horn to call them outside. They took the land transport from the mansion and rode back to the ships in comfort.

The two fighters rose into the air then blasted into open space. Two days later they landed on Nova Prime and began the more pleasant tasks of establishing farms and a temple.

————●————

SEVERAL WEEKS HAD PASSED since the death of the former viceroy. In those weeks Gorda had managed to find a transport ship. He'd scoured the planet for farm equipment and brought it to the place Micha and Edie had chosen for the community farm. Other people had begun to return to Nova as the news of its resurrection spread and all were welcomed.

Micha and Edie sat on the hilltop above their new farm, watching the sunset. He put his arm around her shoulders and pulled her closer. "What's on your mind, my love?" he asked softly.

"Oh, I was just remembering the first time we met. As I watched that ship take off I was so afraid you wouldn't return; that this day would never come."

"I know. Edie, I can't imagine what you went through while waiting for me to return."

"It was Brenna's dreams that held me together."

"Brenna's dreams?"

"She often dreamed of Lessa. She'd tell me about them. They were such wonderful loving dreams, Micha. They were so beautiful. She'd talk and I'd forget that I was in the middle of a war. They made me think I might someday have a love like that if I could just survive until you came back. That is, if you still wanted me."

"Silly girl, one look in those eyes and I thought of little else but the day I could return for you. I just wasn't sure you'd be there."

"Just where did you expect me to be?" she asked with an arched eyebrow at him. "You chose me and I accepted, where else would I be? I'm a farmer's mate, I belong on his farm."

"Yes you do, Edie. And I promise I'll do all in my power to make it a good farm."

"I know you will, my love. I'm a lucky girl." She smiled then kissed him deeply.

Micha sighed with contentment as their lips parted. "Hmm, perhaps we should stay out here under the stars for a while yet," he grinned. "This could be our last chance for a while."

"Oh?"

"Gorda should be back soon with the animals we need."

"Ena and Murtah will soon be back with their children, and Alla is bringing her mate as well?"

"Yes, I believe so."

"Then we are indeed in for some busy days," she purred as she lay back in the grass. "You'd better take advantage while you can."

"Yes Ma'am," he grinned as he tossed aside his tunic and lay down beside her, pulling her into his arms.

Gorda made a few trips to bring farm animals to Nova and more supplies. Ena settled into the business of setting up a household. Life was busy, but sweet and peaceful. Lessa and Norlene had repaired an old temple near Micha's farm and set themselves up there to serve the people of the new and growing community.

Brenna set up a school for the children that had begun to arrive. Slowly, the hard lines around her eyes relaxed and soon she was heard singing again, almost every day. Lessa always smiled and stopped to listen. Soon the new community was ready to begin the first planting. Everyone gathered around while Lessa and Norlene blessed the land. After they'd finished Micha and Edie stepped forward to plant the first seeds to be planted on Nova Prime in over twenty years.

AS MICHA AND EDIE DROPPED the seeds into the freshly turned soil, far away across the galaxy, a man hurried into a luxurious office that said M.J. O'Loran, C.E.O. on the door. The grey haired man behind the desk looked up, annoyance on his face. "What is it?"

"There is news, sir."

"News?"

"News of your daughter, Miss O'Loran. She's alive and well. She's been out in sector nine these past years."

"Sector nine? Tell me she wasn't caught up in the trade wars and sold into slavery."

"No sir, she's escaped that fate. Apparently, she spent a few years working as a dispatcher."

"A dispatcher? I didn't think she had that kind of steel in her. I guess she's her father's daughter after all. Where is she now?"

"She's joined with a Black Witch, and they've returned to Nova Prime. They've cleared the atmosphere somehow and are resettling the planet."

"Nova Prime." He settled back into his plush chair as he absorbed that bit of information.

"What shall we do, Sir?"

"What? Oh, nothing. Take no action at this time. I need to put some thought into this."

The End

\# \# \# \# \#

About the author: I am a spiritual seeker, dog trainer, official Reiki Master and Interior designer, who has turned her hand to writing. I am also an avid chess player, not a great one, but an avid one. I bake, build, knit, blog, and write romantic adventure. I have roamed far and wide for over seventy years in this realm, and I have seen much; some I wish I had not, and a great deal that I would love to see again.

Some days I feel like Bilbo Baggins, for I've been there and come back again. No, I haven't written a book about my wanderings, but much that I have experienced, observed, learned, surmised, or imagined, is woven into the tales I have written. I do hope you enjoy them.

AND NOW FOR A PEEK into the next tale from the Novan series:

Assassin of Nova

by
Prudence MacLeod,
Book Two of the Nova Series

Escape

"When you're fully aware that death stalks you, only then are you truly alive." Rathbone of Urn the Elder.

"I SPARED NO EXPENSE to help you assemble your team, Doctor. You were supposed to give me super soldiers, not dead bodies."

"Mr. O'Loran, Sir, I did try to warn you; we need to hold back a bit with the strength of the mechanical augments. By pushing the boundaries so hard, we made them too strong. Their bodies are tearing themselves apart. Four of the nine are already dead and I doubt the rest can survive more than a few more days."

"This is unfortunate, most unfortunate."

"Sir, with what we've learned from this trial, we can assure you of complete success with the next series."

"Very well. Terminate the rest and start over." The tall man turned and stalked away. "Don't fail me again, Doctor." His voice faded as he stepped into the elevator.

A powerfully built man had been hiding in the shadows, listening, his instincts screaming at him to run. He slipped silently away as those elevator doors closed. He had just heard his death warrant issued, and he didn't plan to stick around for it to be carried out.

As he reached the corridor to the sleeping quarters, he smelled the gas. Taking a deep breath, he held it as he raced through the gas cloud to the locked door at the end of the hallway. A leaping kick tore the door from the hinges and hurled it against the opposite wall. He had only hoped to kick it open; he still wasn't sure of how much additional strength the mechanical augments had given him. He would soon learn.

Two armed soldiers had been stationed on the other side of that door and both had been knocked unconscious. He snatched up their weapons and fled down another corridor.

Suddenly, the alarms sounded and steel blast doors began to close and lock down. He would soon be trapped. A squad of soldiers came out of another corridor. They'd found him. Before they could raise their weapons he was on them. The battle was terrible and swift. Five dead men lay on the floor as he fled on, but he was trapped.

There was only one possible way out; the garbage chute. Without hesitation he plunged in head first. It was quite a drop but a soft, if smelly, landing. He scrambled over to the side of the container and waited. As soon as it was wheeled into the hold of the ship he climbed out and found the air lock. He had barely enough time to get inside before the ship lifted off.

As the ship rose through the atmosphere, the vid screens all over the central cluster of planets came alive with the news. Rathbone of Urn had gone rouge and escaped the authorities. The manhunt was on, but there were few who wanted to encounter the legendary assassin.

At this point, the ship's pilot stepped through a doorway, his eyes on the hand-held vid screen in his palm. He looked up to see a large man, heavily armed standing in front of him. The armed stranger held his finger to his lips in a sign for silence. "You're him, aren't you?" said the pilot, as he lowered the vid screen to his side.

"Him?"

The pilot held out the vid screen and he lowered his weapon as he took it. A glance at the screen told him all he needed to know. He passed it back. "Damned media never gets anything right," he sighed. "Rathbone of Urn, the assassin, is my grandfather."

"So, who're you?"

"Rathbone of Urn, the mechanic."

"Right. So, you're on this scow because...?"

"I have some repairs to make on the refuse planet."

"Of course you do. You'll be staying behind then, right? Because I just unload then return to Elliston Prime."

"That's right, I'll be staying behind."

With a soft chuckle the man put his back against the wall and slid to the floor. He pulled some ration bars from his jacket pocket and tossed one to Rathbone. "Might as well take a load off, Mr. Mechanic. We've got some time to kill."

Rathbone slid to the floor as well, then began to chew thoughtfully on the ration bar. "How many on the ship?" he asked after a long silence.

"Just me," came the reply, "She's all on auto. All I really need to do is takeoff and return landing. Pretty much everything else is automated."

"Can you do manual override?"

"Sure, but why bother? Tell me you're not really going to steal my poor old scow. They'll shoot you down as soon as you hit open space. She's far too slow to outrun the R.I.M. special police."

"I won't steal your ship," chuckled Rathbone. "I just want you to get close enough so I don't break my neck when I hit the ground."

"Fair enough. So, have you got a plan for getting off the refuse planet?"

"Not yet. I take life one step at a time, my friend. They were trying to kill me, so I escaped. Once I'm on the planet I'll look for the best way to take the next step. What can you tell me about this place?"

"Well, you can survive there, if you call it surviving. It was originally terraformed so you can breathe the air and scratch out a living from the soil. There are a few people living there. I'm supposed to report the human rats, as they call them, but I don't."

"Why not?"

"These folk don't do any harm to anybody; they just scavenge what they can from the refuse. If I report them they'd be exterminated."

"Why do you care?"

"I've seen far too many people die for no reason, friend. I won't add to that."

"You're a veteran?"

"Yes. I was flying the ship that wiped out Nova Prime."

"The plague planet?"

"There wasn't any plague, brother. It was a war. Nova rebelled and we gassed the whole damned planet. Everything died, men, women, children, animals, you name it. When my tour was up I got out and bought this old scow. Now I haul garbage. I get paid damn near the same and I can sleep at night. I won't see folks die needlessly again if I can help it."

Rathbone was silent for a while. At length he laid aside his weapons and relaxed fully back against the bulkhead. "Friends call me Rath," he said, as he held out his hand.

"Deke," replied his host, as he accepted the offered hand.

"Deke, why the hell have you not installed a few comfortable chairs for your passengers?"

"There's a chair in the cockpit," chuckled Deke, "but I promise you're more comfortable here on the floor."

Rathbone grinned at that then twisted a bit to ease the pain in his body. "You're carrying wounds," observed Deke.

"Yeah, a few, but I'd wager yours are deeper." Deke just nodded and didn't reply. "Deke, what are my chances of getting back off that refuse heap?"

"Well, I could take you off again, but you'd just end up back on Elliston Prime."

"Not at all where I want to be. Are there any other options?"

"There is a spot where they dump a lot of old useless ships. A good mech-tech with lots of time on his hands might be able to restore an old speeder or some such. There's nothing military there, though."

"A speeder would be more to my liking anyway," sighed Rathbone. "I just want to get back to Urn; to my companion and child. I'll take them out to the rim; find a little backwater planet where I can set up a mechanic's shop and stay out of the way. I just want to live long enough to see my baby girl grow up."

"All right, Rath, I'll set you down an easy hike to the ship scrapyards." Just then an alarm sounded through the ship. "That's the signal to get to work. We're almost there. Come on, we'll go put her on manual and find a soft spot for a landing."

———————◦◦◦———————

RATHBONE STOOD WATCHING the old ship lift off and fade into the evening sky. With a deep sigh he turned to the endless acres of junk piled just behind where he stood. As he turned a ragged woman scurried away from her hiding place, but she stumbled and fell at his feet. Holding out her hands defensively, she cowered there on the ground. "Please don't kill me," she begged.

"Now why would I want to do that?" he asked, a grin playing at the edges of his mouth.

"You're a soldier; soldiers always try to kill us. We hide, but they find and kill most of us."

"I'm not a soldier anymore, so I have no reason to kill you; any of you, so you can all come out of hiding." At that several others stood and brandished crude weapons.

"We won't share the food," declared one man. "There's not enough to feed a man your size. We only grow enough for ourselves."

"Now that presents a problem," replied Rathbone. "You see, if you won't share the food with me, then I have to find my own. The easiest thing would be to eat one of you. Hell, if I'm stuck here long enough, I'll probably have to eat the lot of you."

They were horrified at that. The men edged closer together, fingering their crude weapons. The woman laughed as she regained her feet. "That's the idea, big fella. I'll help you. Let's start with him, he's the fattest." She cackled again, then her voice evened out with a note of command in it. "Of course we'll share the food with him. He's a human being; we will share."

"But Etta..."

"No buts, we share what we have." She turned to Rathbone and stuck out her hand. "I'm Etta of Naith. I'm elected leader of this sorry group of misfits."

"Rathbone of Urn," he grinned as he shook her hand. "I won't rob you folks of your food, Etta; I can look after myself."

"We'll share the food, Rathbone, come on."

She took his hand and led him into a maze of boulders and junk piles. They soon found themselves in the belly of an old cargo ship. It had been made into a rather homey kitchen. The smell of cooking food was everywhere and it was delightful, pulling at him, reminding him he was still alive. "It's all vegetarian, I'm sorry to say," she said. "We don't get a lot of meat around here."

"Oh, why not?"

"It's too big and we have no way to kill it," said one of the men.

"Understood. Old Deke gave me a handful of protein ration bars. If we add those in with that soup we all get one full round meal; what do you say?"

"You'd share your ration bars?" asked the man.

"I told you he was a human being," said Etta. "Let's eat."

The next morning Rathbone set out. It was late in the afternoon when he spotted what he wanted, the hull of an old style speeder. She'd been gutted, but the hull was still sound. He had his ship.

He was returning to the human encampment when he saw the creature. It was a huge mass of fur, fang, and claw, easily weighing over 300 kilos. It charged him and he brought it down with his blaster. The humans came out of hiding then, staring at the dead bear. "That thing could have killed us all and destroyed our home," muttered one man.

"Is it fit to eat?" asked Rathbone.

"Who knows? Let's find out," chuckled Etta, as she appeared with a knife and started skinning out the carcass. "Looks like meat's back on the menu, folks." With a rousing cheer the others pitched in to help.

"You people need to set up defenses," Rathbone observed, as he set aside the bowl he had just emptied for the second time. "You also need ways to catch your meat and protect yourselves."

"Yes, we do," replied Etta. "Will you help us?"

"Sure, if you folks will help me."

"What do you want?" asked one of the men suspiciously.

"I've found the ship I want, but she's been gutted. I'll need help to locate and transport the parts. You folks help me with that and I'll show you how to protect yourselves from the bears, kill them for meat, and hide yourselves from the soldiers. Will that work for you?"

"It will," replied one of the men. "You'll have to teach us first."

"Understood. We can start at first light."

Several weeks later, the small village was completely hidden, both from above and from the ground. There were several escape routes, but the only way in was through several narrow passages. A bear or a big man would have to squeeze to get through and there were traps along the way. For the first time the people felt safe. There were also several deadfalls set up around the surrounding area. There would be meat.

"I'd like to start work on the ship tomorrow," said Rathbone, as they enjoyed an evening meal.

"Fair enough," agreed Etta. "We'll get at it in the morning, right folks?" There was a round of agreement. Everybody knew they owed their current good health and relative prosperity to Rathbone and what he had taught them. They were also in complete awe of his strength as well as his seeming endless knowledge of tactics and stealth.

"Etta, how long have you folks been on this planet anyway?"

"About ten years now," she replied. "We were refugees from a war zone in Sector Six. The Company sent in soldiers to kill everybody in the camp. The bodies were scooped up and put on a refuse carrier then dumped here. Some of us managed to survive.

"That's our story, now how about yours?"

"Much the same," he sighed, as he leaned back on his elbow. "I was a mech-tech stationed on Elliston Prime, but my home, companion, and child were on Urn. When Gen and Ari took sick I couldn't afford the medicines. The military was recruiting for a new program. Cyborg implants. They said they'd pay for the medicines if I volunteered, so I did.

"The implants were way too strong and some of the guys tore themselves apart. I overheard CEO O'Loran tell the surgeon to terminate the rest of us and start over. I fought my way out and escaped on the refuse hauler. The rest you know."

"So that explains the pain I see in your eyes, Rath," sighed Etta. "Your body's tearing itself apart."

"Yes, it is. I don't know how long I'll last. I just want to see Gen and Ari one more time before I self-destruct."

"We'll do all we can to help you with that. What's the plan?"

"Rebuild that speeder and get off this rock. Go home to my family. Do you want to look for a slightly bigger ship, one big enough to take us all off?"

"You'd do that? You'd help us escape?" Etta's tone betrayed the hope they had not dared to allow themselves.

"I will. It should be easier to find parts for a freight hauler than for that speeder anyway. You folks help me build a ship, then we get out of here. You drop me off at Urn and then head out to the rim."

"I'm not going anywhere," declared one man. "You've made this place safe for us. We can survive here. Out there we'll be hunted outlaws again." The argument was on then. In the end about half of them decided to stay, while the rest wanted to go. They all agreed to help as much as they could. It took nearly three years before they managed to get a ship ready for lift off.

Everyone waved as the battered old freight hauler lifted off and wobbled its way out into space. A week later it set down on Urn. Rathbone quickly traded his two blasters for food supplies for the ship then it lifted off again, Captain Etta at the helm and Rathbone's well wishes ringing in her ears.

Three days later, Rathbone stood staring down at the graves of his companion and daughter.

Don't miss out!

Visit the website below and you can sign up to receive emails whenever Prudence MacLeod publishes a new book. There's no charge and no obligation.

https://books2read.com/r/B-A-ZKBBB-RBURC

BOOKS 2 READ

Connecting independent readers to independent writers.

Also by Prudence MacLeod

Forgotten Worlds
Suvi
Echo of the Past
Survivors
Ship
Fleet
Unite
IGEN
T.E.N.

Nova series
Novan Witch
Assassin of Nova
Beyond Nova
Claimstake
Red Nova

Watch for more at https://www.prudencemacleod.com/.

Telling a story is like knitting a sweater. Start with a ball of possibilities, pull out one small thread and begin. With luck and patience you will create something quite wonderful.

About the Author

On a far off windswept island Jennifer Crandall sits with her dogs and cats creating fantastic stories for all to enjoy. She publishes as JL Crandall, Prudence MacLeod, and Jenni Leigh.

Read more at https://www.prudencemacleod.com/.